LOVERS' CRESCENT

THE FIRST LUNAR LOVESCAPE NOVEL

ESSIE POWERS

ENTRY CLEARANCE

*L*ouise Williams gripped her cross-chest straps tightly. The constant, eardrum-piercing screech of the reverse thrusters was nearly unbearable, even from within the confines of her helmet; even despite the noise-cancelling technology of her earbuds.

But, as bad as the sound was, the vibrations were worse.

In fact, the whole ordeal was driving her beyond the edge of despair. Although she had never been remotely afraid of flying, she had to admit that something about space travel did make her nerves jangle . . . even now as she was nearing the end of the sixteen-hour journey.

Even as they descended to the surface of the Moon.

For so long she had dreamed about this moment. She had woken in cool, feverish sweats in the middle of the night *just thinking* about the surface of the Moon. About how it would feel to finally walk upon its fine, chalky dust. And now she couldn't do anything but squeeze her eyes shut and hope it would all be over as soon as possible; as if she was a nine-year-old girl trapped in the body of a twenty-eight-year-old woman.

She supposed, in some ways, she was . . .

How she had needed to start all over again.

How she was 'running away' from her problems—just like her mother had termed it.

Louise squeezed the cross-chest straps tighter still. The sharp edges of the straps dug into the fleshy portions of her palms. She held on so tightly that it felt as if her scuffed and chipped fingernails might split right down the middle.

Hoping to mitigate this unpleasant sensation she sunk her teeth into her lower lip.

But it did no good.

It only made her heart beat more strongly in her ears. It only brought a bitter, coppery taste of blood onto the tip of her tongue. Her whole body, it seemed, was on the point of shutting down. She was on the point of giving herself up to some sort of nineteenth-century swoon . . .

The sudden jerk of the Lander brought her back to reality.

It took her stomach a few seconds to catch up with her brain.

Her eyes snapped open—*seemingly of themselves*—and she peered out of a porthole.

She observed the articulated legs, awkwardly jutting out of the Lander's spherical body.

The legs made the Lander seem like some deeply improbable, mechanical space spider . . . a space spider making a less-than-graceful landing from some great height.

The Lander bucked upward, back down.

Finding its balance.

And then, all of a sudden, everything was still.

Everything *stopped.*

The engines were gone.

The constant vibrations, too.

Only the ringing in her ears remained.

She took in the lunar plains:

Rutted. Uneven.

Roaming for kilometres uncountable to the human eye.

This was it . . . this was her new home . . . at least for the duration of her eighteen-month contract with Celestial Stays; the sole provider of lunar hospitality.

She breathed in deeply.

She tore her eyes away from the porthole.

Turned them back to her fellow passengers.

The fifteen others sat side by side about the periphery of the lunar Lander.

Facing into her.

All of them, like her, blinking away their traveller's daze.

Coming to terms with their new surroundings.

Their new situation.

She couldn't shake that comparison she'd made to herself when she'd first set foot in the lunar Lander, about how it seemed like a fairground ride . . . one of those rides which threw the punters upward, then down again at astonishing speeds.

The landing hadn't been much different to a fairground ride . . .

Although the destination was, surely, beyond any of their wildest dreams.

Half a dozen evenly spaced chimes sounded in her earbuds.

She recognised those chimes, of course.

They were Celestial Stays' unmistakable jingle; the sound which any man, woman or child on Earth could reproduce at the drop of a hat. It was the calling card that'd been heard on advertisements, news reports, for all of Louise's life.

3

And now, finally, she would get to see what all the fuss was about.

The chimes gave way to a soothing, gender- and accent-neutral voice.

"Welcome to the Moon. Passengers are to remain seated until further instruction."

What the voice believed them capable of—with the automatic-locking chest straps still harnessing them firmly in their seats—Louise could only imagine.

Louise couldn't take her eyes off the view stretching out above her, beyond her helmet visor and beyond the glass roof of the lunar rover—or 'Rover', as they were more often simply referred to.

The famous Celestial Stays Dome.

It was just as easily recognised in monographed silhouette as in four-dimensional full-detail.

Again, as with the trademark, half dozen chimes, the outline of the Dome was etched into the mind of every man, woman or child of Earth.

She stared and stared and stared.

To the buildings nestled within.

The leafy avenues.

The spurting fountains.

The bustling activity.

It was only when she heard the voice in her ear once again that she brought her attention back to her immediate surroundings. To the automated Rover.

From the wide-eyed, opened-mouthed expressions of her travelling companions, she could see that the sight of the Celestial Stays Dome had had a similar effect on them.

"Next stop, Celestial Stays Employee Initiation—via Entry Clearance."

The Rover continued its unchecked, steady progress to the airlock.

The cursive initials of 'Celestial Stays'—*C.S.*—swept across the double doors before them.

Having left the Rover behind, Louise just stood and stared.

In how many pictures—how many *films*?—had she absorbed this sight?

It was as if she was standing before the Gates of Heaven themselves . . . with all the wonder and intrigue that implied.

Bereft of her helmet—as the rest of her companions were—her blond hair bunched into an untidy bun, she watched the doors unfold themselves.

She knew, as with the rest of the voyage, there would be no preventing her mouth's natural tendency to flop open in disbelief.

Still, that didn't seem to matter all that much.

Nobody was looking at *one another*, after all.

They were all fixed on what lay ahead.

She had to remind herself to breathe. And, when she did so, she found her mind whipping her back to the training sessions she had been through on Earth. How she had been told that the air within the Dome would be different to that which she was used to . . . different to the thickly oxygenated stuff she'd got used to on the trip here. She needed to breathe shallowly at first—guard against getting a light head. She wasn't completely certain whether it was because of the quality of the air or the awe at being here—*on the Moon!*—which made her feel a touch dizzy.

The doors were wide open now.

All sixteen of them stood and stared at the gap.

Like a mirror image, another sixteen people stood on the other side of the door staring back at them.

Their overalls were the royal-blue of Celestial Stays; somewhat grander than the dirty-grey flight overalls which Louise and the others had all worn on the journey here.

A female member of the group with flowing red hair took a step forward.

Louise immediately noted the glittering, golden Supervisor's patch on the breast pocket of her overalls. The others behind the Supervisor wore silver, Guardian patches.

As Louise had been informed during employee briefing back down on Earth, Celestial Stays was organised into five distinct Divisions: Hospitality, Tourism, Security, Catering and Human Resources.

Each of those Divisions was managed by a Supervisor who—in turn—had Guardians beneath them to help carry out day-to-day orders.

What most surprised Louise about the Supervisor wasn't that— to anybody with eyes—she was stunningly beautiful, but that she couldn't be much older than thirty years old.

Since Celestial Stays only took on employees older than twenty-one, and since they only allowed for eighteen months of service at a time followed by eighteen months working Earthside —*for medical reasons*—the Supervisor couldn't have gone through more than three rotations on Luna.

And yet in that time she'd become one of the most senior members of the Celestial Stays team.

With a simple *snap* of her fingers, the Supervisor sent the fifteen Guardians marching toward Louise and her soon-to-be colleagues. Louise noted that the Guardians were of all ages, although perhaps on average more firmly stacked toward the fifty-year mark: the cut-off for lunar service.

Louise watched on—impotently—as Guardians descended upon each of her companions in turn.

It didn't take her long to realise that there wasn't going to be a Guardian for her.

That they had all run out.

Acting on impulse more than anything else, she turned her attention to the Supervisor, and found herself on the receiving end of a burning, emerald-green stare.

Feeling a lump forming in her throat, Louise could only observe as the Supervisor struck up a wry smile and stepped toward her. It took Louise a couple of moments before she noticed the hand sticking into her belly. Somewhat beleaguered, she gripped the Supervisor's hand and felt each and every one of the muscles in her hand being crushed.

"Supervisor Angliss," the Supervisor muttered, in what Louise recognised to be a dry Australian accent. "Human Resources."

"Louise," she managed to get out. "Louise Williams. Uh," she paused for a second or so, "I think I'm assigned to Hospitality—"

The Supervisor—Supervisor *Angliss*—turned away from her, apparently distracted by something or other. When Louise followed her gaze, she saw that one of the Guardians was looking beleaguered, calling out in Angliss's direction.

Angliss turned back into Louise. "One second, blue eyes," she said, her tone hurried, business-like; the term of endearment seeming wildly out of place.

Louise took in the scene, her fellow new-recruit.

It was a woman with tanned skin; sleek, nut-brown hair cropped short and neatly tucked into a bun. She was wide-eyed and, apparently, taken off guard by whatever the trouble was.

Louise overheard fragments of the conversation.

". . . Says she's assigned to Tourism," the Guardian explained. "Only I can't find any record on the Link."

Louise observed Angliss, and watched on as she reached up and pressed a finger to her inner-ear, clearly consulting the Link for the information she required.

Without uttering a word—not *needing* to utter a word, having, like everybody else on Earth, a neural transmitter located in her frontal lobe—she turned back to the Guardian, the stunned new-recruit, and gave a nod coupled with a pert, half-second-long smile.

As Angliss trod back toward her, Louise overheard the Guardian explaining to the new-recruit that, "Everything was fine", and that she was, "All signed-up and ready to go".

Louise was so immersed by the scene that she almost missed the smart *click* of fingers as Angliss passed her by; the almost inaudibly uttered, "This way, blue eyes."

Louise flashed a final glance to the brown-haired woman, catching her eye for a moment.

The two of them exchanged a nervous smile and Louise just about had time to catch sight of the nametag sewn onto the pocket of her overalls:

K. SINGH

Apparently taking too long, another *click* of fingers brought Louise back to the present.

She set off at a quick pace, jogging to catch up with Angliss's swiftly disappearing heels.

They passed through several glass corridors, giving a view down onto the entirety of the resort; the whole Celestial Stays complex, located in the southern crater of the Moon.

Still, it didn't seem real to Louise.

She took in the details through some sort of a haze.

She looked over the cylindrical, golden glass tower which was the Lunar Grand; the six-star hotel used as the centrepiece in so many aspirations, so many dreams:

One day, dear, in our suite at the Lunar Grand. When we eat lunar-grown strawberries off a silver platter all served with thick, Earth-sourced cream. One day, my dear.

Louise couldn't help but replay the line from some cheesy film in her head.

Further across the Celestial Stays complex, she made out the Stellar Tide Casino; its squat, rectangular building. Like the other buildings, it had a golden hue to it. She recalled hearing that it had been the architect's desire to reflect the protective bronze foil of NASA's famed lunar lander. Some thought it corny, but Louise quite liked the effect. It drew everything together, giving the out-of-place, human constructions a much-needed touch of grace.

Further away still, she could make out the squirly, S-shaped Armstrong Archive; the library and reference centre which would feature prominently during any guest's stay.

It was located beside the compact, homey Orbital Café . . . again so often the spark for a romantic encounter, or else the ending point for a turbulent affair.

Finally, Louise took in the Crescent Gardens which ran—as

their name suggested—through the entire Celestial Stays resort in the form of a crescent Moon.

The greenery from the Gardens twisted up toward the top of the Dome, in some places making contact with the glass. Straining to be closer to the sun . . . straining to be closer to Earth.

She watched people moving about in Personal Transporters —*PEARS*—from place to place.

The bubble-like shapes of the vehicles weaved through the air on their unseen, Link-controlled pathways.

"This building here's Entry Clearance," Angliss said, her words carrying over her shoulder.

Realising that Angliss was getting away from her again, Louise quickened her pace, turning her attention away from the incredible sight of the Celestial Stays complex.

"You came through the Airlock then got dumped in the Rover Pool." She jabbed her finger into her inner-ear, tilted her head to one side slightly, then seemed to go faster still. "That's where we met up with you. Where we just came from."

"Uh . . . ," Louise just about got out, before noticing that Angliss had her finger jabbed into her inner-ear again—sending off another message or else consulting with the Link.

As they continued on, Louise thought it odd that she had ended up with a Supervisor; and the Supervisor of Human Resources, no less.

What made her so special?

Why hadn't she been paired with a Guardian like the others?

As if reading her mind, Angliss spoke again over her shoulder, her relentless pace never slowing for so much as a second. "Guardian who was meant to meet you from Hospitality was taken ill this morning at Oh-Three-Hundred Hours."

It took Louise a moment to realise that Angliss was saying that the Guardian meant to meet with her had been taken ill at three o'clock that morning.

"You've been assigned to the Crescent Gardens, blue eyes, that's where I'm taking you now. After you've gone through Initiation Protocol." She shook her head and, finally, glanced back over her shoulder at Louise. "Can you believe that everybody was all tied up this morning? That there wasn't anybody else to take you through Initiation?"

More than anything, Louise wanted to bring up the topic of that 'blue eyes' nickname—it was already beginning to wear—but it was all she could do to get out a hurried, "No" before Angliss seized her by the crook of her elbow and jerked her through a steadily opening door.

The door hardly had time to sweep out of sight before they were standing on the other side.

Although there was no window looking out from this room, Louise was rendered speechless by the sight all the same. She took in the row-upon-row of machines—*droids*—going through all manner of testing procedures with those who Louise recognised as being fellow new-recruits. She noticed—off to the other end of the area—that there was a whole automated rack of royal-blue overalls just ready to be fitted to new employees.

Angliss continued to guide Louise onward, her fingers digging—*a touch painfully*—into her skin. She whipped Louise through the droids which in turn checked respiration, scanned her muscular structure, and finally, without warning, drew blood.

Louise rubbed at the spot on her forearm where the droid had seen fit to stick her with the needle.

As Angliss led her away from the droids, Louise couldn't help but notice that she was the first of the new recruits to make it through Entry Clearance; that she would be the first of them to be fitted for her new overalls.

Louise supposed that Angliss had this whole 'Initiation Protocol' down to something like a science; well accustomed to leading green recruits through the process in an efficient manner which would allow her to get on with the rest of her day . . . to get on with *important* matters.

In no time at all, Louise had somehow shucked her flight overalls and replaced them with the standard-issue royal-blues. She noted, already, that there was a nametag—L. WILLIAMS—sewn onto the pocket of the overall. As with her flight overalls, the flag of her country of origin was stamped beside her name; the proud red, white and blue of the Union Jack. If Louise hadn't before identified Angliss as a no-nonsense Aussie from her accent, she could easily have done so from the flag beside her name.

Before Louise really knew what was happening, Angliss was telling her to watch her head as the visor of a Personal Transporter whirred downward.

Louise was glad to find a seat beneath her bottom, and promptly allowed herself to sink down into the cool, pleasantly strained leather.

Staring out through the visor, Angliss spoke from the corner of her mouth. "Guess you know from stuff down on Earth that Personal Transporters are known as PEARS, huh?"

Louise didn't even have time to nod, *Yes*, she *did* know that . . .

"Yeah," Angliss went on, somehow finding time to jab her inner-ear again, sending off another message to the Link, "I think of them more like *mozzies*—you know what a *mozzie* is, don't you, blue eyes?"

"A mosquito," Louise replied.

"Damn right," Angliss shot back. "Bloody, god-awful, bastard things."

Louise couldn't help herself dizzily wondering if Angliss might have some long-ago, not-so-repressed childhood trauma surrounding mosquitoes.

Again, though, there was no time to ask, because the Personal Transporter—the *PEAR*—sped inches above the lunar surface, careening toward the greenery which was the Crescent Gardens.

2

THE CRESCENT GARDENS

*L*ouise *was able* to count her heartbeats—all five of them—before the PEAR came to a lazy halt on the illuminated landing pad outside the entrance to the Crescent Gardens.

When they arrived, Angliss leaped up out of her seat, in perfect time with the lifting of the PEAR's visor, as if the PEAR was well-aware of Angliss's penchant for speed, and only too glad to get out of the way lest it come to harm.

Louise's landing was less elegant as she nearly tripped over the side of the PEAR, but she somehow stumbled her way back into balance before causing herself any harm.

This time, Angliss didn't see fit to grab physical hold of Louise —a fact which she was inordinately happy about—and it was a comparably leisurely walk along the gravel pathway, through the sprawling greenery, toward a building rising tall and proud out of the landscape.

A red laser force field blocked the entrance marked RESTRICTED but Angliss walked through the barrier as if it wasn't there at all; so nonchalant that she saw fit to issue yet more orders, her finger sticking into her inner-ear, as she went.

Louise, feeling somewhat *less* sure about walking through what looked to be a very solid force field, hung back.

Now on the other side of the force field, Angliss turned around, looked over her shoulder at Louise. Then she snapped her fingers again, this time not necessarily as an order, but more as if some vital detail had simply happened to slip her mind.

Again, she reached up and inserted her finger into her inner-ear.

"I'm authenticating your connection to the Link now," she said, referring to Louise's own direct neural connection to the Celestial Stays Link.

Sure enough, Louise heard those half dozen familiar chimes of Celestial Stays, and then, for a couple of seconds, witnessed the silhouetted watermark of the Celestial Stays logo—*the Dome*—mottling her vision. She heard the simple, crisp, clear status read-out, spoken in that same soft, gender- and accent-neutral tone from before:

ONLINE

This was followed by an equally simple declaration:

HOSPITALITY ACCESS GRANTED: CRESCENT GARDENS LEVEL 1

"That'll do for now," Angliss replied, as if she'd heard these read-outs as clearly as Louise had heard them from within the realms of her own skull. "Come on," she added, making off again, into the depths of the building.

Feeling somewhat taken aback, and not a little overwhelmed, Louise followed.

———

As Louise trod through the corridors, she found herself slightly overcome by the odour of earth.

It was all around her, almost as if she had gone deep underground.

She had never been much of a fan of the Great Outdoors, as some of its more ardent fans would term it; she'd always thought she could experience just as much through a Zito Entertainment Unit.

A Zito gave her all five senses plus a four-dimensional rendering of just about anything she—or *anybody* else—could imagine.

Then again, wasn't there something to be said for seeing things in the *real* world?

Wasn't that the reason why she'd decided she *had* to come to the Moon rather than just be contented with some Zito's rendering of the same?

She noted that the scent of earth—the kind of reverence which accompanied their surroundings—had had a similar effect on Angliss

She had slowed her pace. She hadn't reached up to her inner-ear to snap off another command for what felt like an eternity.

Slowly, Louise recognised another smell lingering on the air, beyond that of the earth.

Flowers.

Which ones, again, she couldn't be absolutely sure . . . but flowers, and fruits, and vegetables, it all had the same sentimental effect on her.

Angliss tilted her head back slightly, and then called out through the building. "Hello? Anyone home?"

The building was dark, with only a few dim lights flickering away. Through the gloom, Louise could just about make out doorways, and the decorated, flowery patterns on the walls; all of it sourced and programmed by the Link.

Through the darkness, she heard a muted response.

Angliss, cocking her head like a dog to a high-pitched whistle, tracked the reply.

Finally, she led Louise through a doorway and into a—*slightly better lit*—room.

There Louise took in the metal tables, and the read-out screens hanging in mid-air, showing off various graphs and colourful numbers crawling along—one after the other.

On the other side of the room, she noticed a man. He wore a lab coat over his Celestial Stays overalls. He was perusing a microscope.

Now Louise could smell something else in the air; the smell of coffee mingled in with that unmistakable *masculine* scent of hard work. Strangely, she felt a fizzle at the base of her gut.

It had been a long time since she had felt something like that; a long time *indeed*.

Angliss coughed.

The man in the lab coat straightened up all of a sudden, bumping his head on a pipe which jutted down from the ceiling. With a muffled swearword followed by a hissing *suck* of his teeth, he turned to face them through the gloom, rubbing his head and grimacing.

"Oh, it's you," Angliss said, then arched an eyebrow. "Busy?"

"Uh . . ." the man replied.

"Wendy not out of her sickbed yet?"

"Said she's on her way—few more minutes yet."

Angliss sighed.

Apparently rendered speechless for the time being, the man glanced back at what he'd been doing at the microscope. After a few seconds, he turned, wearing a vaguely embarrassed expression. "I'll get the lights, shall I?"

With a simple jab of his inner-ear, a mechanical whine sounded and then fluorescent, strip lights blinked on all around them, flooding the room with a bright, white glow.

For the first time Louise could make out the man properly.

Like the new recruit Louise had seen back at Entry Clearance, he had brown skin. He also had proud, pinched cheeks. He had curly black hair streaked with a couple of scraps of silver.

She supposed he was about five years older than she was.

A pair of thick-rimmed glasses were nearly lost among his thick hair, in the same way a garden hose becomes lost in overgrown tufts of grass. Faint stubble softened his firm jawline. She caught a flash of his nametag on the royal-blue overalls he wore beneath his lab coat:

N. GARCIA

Although she could just about make out the flag beside the man's name—a geometric, red, blue and white design with a golden sun to the left—she couldn't identify his country of origin right away. To be quite honest, she was somewhat distracted by the sculpted lines of the man's abdomen and pectoral muscles which showed through his tight-fitting overalls.

Realising that her mind had floated miles away, she tuned back into what was going on around her. She realised that Angliss was speaking again.

"New one for you, García," Angliss said.

Finally, for what seemed like the first time, he looked to her.

And Louise felt her heart flutter up to her throat.

For what must've been only several seconds—but which felt like several *hours*—she lost herself in his soft, cool, bronze-green eyes. They were liquid, constantly on the move, never able to be pinned down. It seemed as if his drooping, slightly sleepy eyelids were just some ploy—*a sleight of hand*—to keep her unaware of the danger, the *real* danger, which lurked just beneath.

He was the first to look away.

He glanced back to his microscope, though this time a little distractedly.

"You'll help her settle in?" Angliss said. "You won't do anything to damage her before the grownup arrives?"

"Uh-huh," the man—*García*—replied, his mind obviously elsewhere.

As if it would facilitate her departure, he turned back to Angliss and flashed a brief smile; a smile filled with pearly-white teeth that almost glittered as much as the silver badges Guardians wore.

"Good," Angliss replied, shortly, in a no-nonsense manner.

Louise waited. And waited. Expected Angliss to take her leave. As she had been so clearly wanting to do throughout their brief acquaintanceship.

But she hung back, apparently uncertain of something.

Finally, she turned into Louise, flashed another smile. This time there was something different about her smile; something more *subtle* about it.

Some kind of . . . vulnerability?

If vulnerability *was* what Louise had really seen, then it was gone as soon as she noticed it, and she found herself, once again, being whisked away from the scene held tightly beneath Angliss's very strong wing. "A quick word, blue eyes."

Once they were out in the corridor—now flooded with even, clinical, *laboratory* light—Angliss glanced around her to make sure they were really alone, and then leaned into Louise, dropping the tone of her voice to conspiratorial levels.

"Look," Angliss said, "I want to admit to something."

"What?" Louise replied.

Angliss blinked a pair of times, stared back into Louise's eyes, and then looked away again. Finally, she said, "You didn't *really* think that this is normal procedure; that a Supervisor would be put into place to bring along a new recruit just because someone was off sick? Just because Wendy came down with something this morning?"

Louise's chest tightened.

Angliss continued, "I looked into your file—into your *background*."

A slight dizziness struck Louise.

No, this couldn't be happening.

Not now.

Not here.

So far away . . .

Not even on the same planet any longer.

Not even . . .

But Angliss kept speaking.

"I couldn't help noticing your employment history, although you neglected to include the information as part of your application." She cocked her head to one side, smiled wryly. "That you were so high up at Humble Associates." Her smiled widened. "I don't see why you would keep something like that from a future employer . . . especially one such as Celestial Stays . . . why"—again

Angliss glanced over her shoulder, then dropped her voice down even further, to a husky whisper—"you might angle your way into a Supervisor's job after a couple of rotations." She paused—a long *pregnant* pause. "Just like I did," she added, finally.

Louise felt as if she was sinking, as if she might be dropping right down through the fine dust which covered the Moon's surface; as if she might keep on going until she fell out through the bottom, and drifted on off into outer space.

She looked to Angliss, lips parted, unable to reply.

Her voice died in her throat.

"Don't worry," Angliss said, with her widest smile yet. "Your secret's safe with me, blue eyes." She tapped her nose with the same finger she used so often to trigger an order with her inner-ear. As she made her way past Louise, she muttered a parting word over her shoulder. "Let me know if you change your mind—if you decide that menial labour isn't for you."

And, with that, Angliss disappeared off down the corridor.

Leaving Louise to her thoughts.

Leaving Louise to the realisation that she would never escape.

Never.

3

INITIATION PROTOCOLS

Louise was in some kind of a haze when she returned to the laboratory where she'd been presented to the man; to N. GARCIA. Although she was on the Moon, her brain had deserted her . . . it had taken the leap and travelled all the way back to Earth.

When she did set foot back inside the brightly lit room, and when she noticed N. GARCIA sat on the edge of one of the metal examination tables sipping on his coffee, her heart beat faster. The combination of past thoughts—past *feelings*—and those which now overcame her in the present moment. She did her best to flush away the past.

She put on a smile.

"Uh, hi," she got out.

N. GARCIA smiled back at her, a little awkwardly, but with genuine warmth. He shifted his weight off the edge of the table, slugged back the remainder of his coffee, and then trod toward

her. Holding his finished cup of coffee down at his side, he held
out his hand for her to shake. "Name's Njhay," he said.

" 'En-jay' ?" Louise replied, once again arrested by those
bronze-green eyes.

While Angliss's handshake had been firm, professional . . .
painful . . . Njhay's handshake, although it displayed strength, was
tender, almost . . . *playful?*

"Sure," he replied, still smiling, "it's spelled N-J-H-A-Y. *Njhay.*"

Feeling herself begin to tremble, she broke off the handshake.
She turned away from him, and then glanced about the laboratory.
"So," she said, "what do you get up to here?"

Njhay turned side on to take in the scene, as if he hadn't seen
this room before in all his life. "A great deal, but mostly trying to
work out how to grow stuff on the Moon." He turned back to her,
smiling gently. Then he reached up for his glasses, tugged them
down out of his wild hair, set them on the bridge of his nose and
eyed her through the thick lenses. "I'm sorry," he said, "I didn't get
your name, L. WILLIAMS."

Feeling somewhat ditzy, Louise tilted her head down to her
nametag, as if she didn't quite believe what it said. She glanced
back up at him.

Smiled.

"It's Louise," she finally got out.

"Huh," Njhay replied, as if surprised.

"What?"

Njhay held her gaze for another few long seconds then he
shook his head. "Nothing," he said. "Just some . . . I don't know . . .
déjà vu, I guess. British?"

"That's right."

He smiled lightly. "Could tell from the accent." He indicated the flag beside his own nametag. "Filipino," he stated, and then, "London?"

Louise shook her head. "Bristol."

"Batangas City."

Louise searched her mind and then berated herself for not being able to say anything about Njhay's hometown. She had never been the best at geography, even when, in her past job, she had been compelled to travel.

Njhay's smile widened. "It's a port."

"Ah," Louise replied, thinking on her feet. "Bristol has a . . . uh, bridge."

Njhay chuckled, quick, spontaneous and boyish. When he laughed, all the skin around his eyes creased up, and his eyes narrowed so that they almost closed.

Louise did her best to laugh along, but she mainly just blushed.

Soon silence draped down over the laboratory.

Louise always felt uncomfortable with silence.

So she broke it.

"She's really something, huh?"

Sinking his teeth into his lower lip, Njhay seemed to be miles away. His previous joviality had dissipated. Finally he returned to the present moment with a bump, blinking twice. "Who . . . Angliss?"

"Yeah. And I can't tell you how sick I am of being called 'blue eyes.'"

Njhay gave a slight shrug. A trace of his former smile returned. "That's nothing, she called me 'Specky' till she decided I wasn't a threat." He pointed to the glasses perched on his nose.

"She thinks I'm a threat?"

"I guess she doesn't know what to think. Not quite yet." He glanced past her, to the doorway. "You'll get used to Angliss. She's ambitious, that's all—Supervisors are always that way. Kind of the reason why they *become* Supervisors."

Louise nodded to Njhay's Celestial Stays overalls beneath his lab coat. "I didn't notice a Guardian badge there."

Njhay coloured slightly. "Yeah, well, some of us know how to play the game better than others." He shrugged. "Some of us don't want to play the game at all."

Louise felt the urge to prod at that little morsel, that resentment clearly bubbling just below the surface. She wondered what Njhay's beef with Angliss might be.

"Listen," Njhay said, hooking his thumb over his shoulder, "I should be getting back to my studies." He reached up, adjusted his glasses over the bridge of his nose once more. "Whenever somebody catches me in the middle of something my mind's always running elsewhere—always still stuck on the work I was doing, if you see what I mean?"

Louise pressed her lips together in a polite smile, getting another glimpse of those unfathomable, bronze-green eyes. He gave her the hint of a smile as he turned his back to her, and—*true to his word*—sat back down at his microscope.

Louise had only been standing where she was for a matter of moments when a voice sounded over her shoulder.

"Williams? Louise Williams?"

Louise turned.

A woman stood in the doorway.

She had silver hair.

Louise's gaze instantly settled on the silver Guardian's badge which was stitched onto the pocket of the woman's royal-blue overalls.

"That's me," Louise said, flashing a final glance back at Njhay.

True to his word, he was wrapped up in his work; his eye glued to his microscope.

"This way, please," the woman said, shifting a look in Njhay's direction before fastening her attention back onto Louise.

Not wishing to argue, Louise set off after the woman.

Although it was hard to do, she forced herself not to look back at Njhay.

The last thing she needed right now—now that she had escaped Earth—was to find herself caught in the talons of some mysterious stranger.

"I'm Wendy," the woman announced, smartly, as they turned another of the apparently endless corners. "Zimbabwe," she added, as if this explained something.

At the very least it explained the green, yellow, red and black striped flag on her breast pocket.

From a quick glance at Wendy's nametag, Louise saw her surname was Flowme.

As they walked along, Louise analysed the woman.

She had a near-flawless complexion; a deeply feminine, tightly coiled figure. Despite her outward, vital appearance, Louise decided that the woman had to be nearing the fifty-year-old cut-off for serving on Luna . . . though it would've been imprudent to ask.

"Sorry about this morning," she said, speaking in an accent which reminded Louise of South African English. "I had some shellfish last night." She paused briefly, reaching out and pressing her palm just below Louise's ribcage so that she had no option but to stop too.

Wendy puffed out her cheeks, smiled.

Louise smiled along.

"Shellfish. On the Moon. *Really*," Wendy said, carrying on. "You have *no* idea." She shook her head. "Never again."

Eventually, they left the building behind, emerging out into the cool, crisp air of the Crescent Gardens.

Despite her verdant surroundings—the flowers of hundreds of colours which sprouted out from all places—Louise couldn't help but feel that there was something missing here; what it was exactly, she couldn't quite put her finger on . . .

When she turned to Wendy, she saw that she was eyeing her closely, and smiling. "No birdsong," Wendy said. "I know, it gets me every time—doesn't feel *natural*, does it?"

Louise glanced around. "I don't suppose there's all that much natural about growing flowers on the Moon."

Wendy held her finger to her lips in a mock-serious manner. "Shh," she said. "Don't say that too loud." She pointed about them. "The plants have *ears*."

Louise laughed.

Wendy led her onward, past the flowerbeds. "Hydrangeas," Wendy explained, pointing out the blue, pink and white flowers as they passed by. "Celestial Stays has a certain scientific commitment as part of their lease on the southern crater of the Moon. Most of the initial investment went into the Armstrong Archive." She stopped dead. "You haven't visited yet, have you?"

Since there didn't seem to be a chance of getting a word in edgeways, Louise had to content herself with a simple shake of her head.

Wendy went on, "To begin with I don't mind saying that the Crescent Gardens weren't much more than a boxy greenhouse. But it didn't take much time for that to change. When the higher-ups in Hospitality saw what a hit it was with the guests they decided to expand, and, well . . ."

Wendy stretched her arms out to indicate the expansive gardens as far as the eye could see. From her vantage point, Louise could only just make out the tops of the surrounding buildings: the Lunar Grand, the Stellar Tide Casino and the Armstrong Archive.

Beyond that there was only the Dome; and the blackness of space.

It was strange—*so strange*.

They walked on, Wendy apparently taking the opportunity to catch her breath.

Finally, Wendy came to a halt. "Well," she said, "I think you've seen enough." She made a circling motion with her wrist in the air, as if to indicate that the Gardens continued on in a similar manner for a long while yet. "Lilies, peas, buttercups, magnolias, roses, cacti, orchids—one of Njhay's more successful ventures"—she drew breath—"*All* sorts."

There was a pause. Louise took her opportunity. "So," she said, "what's going to be my job?"

Wendy smiled wide and proud. "Watering, weeding, plucking, chopping, pruning . . . you don't *mind* getting your hands dirty, do you?"

Louise shook her head, and she couldn't help smiling back.

There was something about Wendy's enthusiastic manner that was strangely infectious.

"But that can all wait for the time being," Wendy said. "I suppose you're dying to see what your living arrangements are going to be like for the next year and a half."

Before Louise had so much as a chance to reply, Wendy was off again, rattling off some explanation about going to catch a PEAR.

They arrived at the location known as the Basements, toward the fringe of the Celestial Stays Dome. As they'd swept into the landing pad, Louise had soon realised how it had earned that name.

Unlike the other buildings within the Celestial Stays Dome, only about half a floor of the Basements protruded above the lunar surface. Louise certainly never would've picked it out of the skyline while she'd been back at Entry Clearance unless she'd had it pointed out for her.

She supposed that—as with most service industries—'out of sight, out of mind', was an adage which was strictly applied.

In fact, the top floor of the Basements consisted only of a brief, deserted lounge. Its only purpose appeared to be somewhere to place the lift which descended beneath the lunar surface.

Wendy guided Louise into the lift and the two of them took it down to—what Louise saw to be—Level B5. This, Louise guessed, was to be her home for the foreseeable future.

The décor throughout Level B5 was Spartan, although the walls had at least been thoughtfully programmed with various images of swirling galaxies and distant star systems.

Wendy seemed to know the place back to front.

She had no trouble guiding Louise to her bedroom; Room B5-7.

And although the stainless steel door wasn't as much welcoming as it was functional, Louise was pleasantly surprised by the setup within. How there was a sizeable bed, a simple, but generous en suite, and an ample wardrobe . . . stuffed full with royal-blue overalls and—she noticed—a freshly cleaned, dirty-grey set of flight overalls; for the return journey?

Although there wasn't a window—it being five and a half floors beneath the lunar surface—the wallpaper was programmed to show off 'soothing' sights.

At present it was set to a mountainous forest glistening with morning dew.

"Well," Wendy said, hands on hips. "There's some other stuff about here, too; but most importantly there's the canteen. You want to go take a look?"

Still feeling overwhelmed by all that had happened since her arrival, Louise couldn't quite find her voice right away. It surprised her that, when she did find her voice, it was not to ask a pragmatic question about what would become her day-to-day routine.

"Don't Angliss and Njhay get on?"

Wendy blinked several times, apparently just as taken off guard as Louise was for having had the gall to ask it. She soon shrugged her shoulders, though. "Listen," she said, "I'm on my final lunar rotation—this will be my last six months on the Moon. During these eight rotations I've seen all sorts, been witness to all *kinds* of things, seen this Dome go from what it was decades ago to what it is now. What *hasn't* changed, though, is the same old conflict that —probably since time immemorial—has run and run and run."

"And what conflict's that?" Louise put in, feeling a little blunt.

At least she had the excuse of space travel to explain away her ditziness.

"Why, the conflict between Commerce and Science." Wendy made to interlock her fingers but instead ended up forming fists. She bumped them into one another. "Njhay sees himself as advancing some sort of scientific frontier while Angliss believes that the single greatest business opportunity known to mankind has sprung into existence . . . and neither one, really, wants anything to do with the other." She allowed her arms to fall back down by her sides. "*Conflict*," she added, with a note of finality. "An 'uneasy compromise', if I could put it that way."

Louise took a second to absorb this, and then said, "Although the Gardens *are* beautiful, they wouldn't exist if there wasn't any form of funding them—if someone hadn't worked out a model to bring money to the Moon."

Wendy winked. "I think we're going to get on just fine, you and I. Now," she said, heading for the exit, "I'll leave you to freshen up —dinner's at eight-hundred hours *sharp*."

"Wait," Louise said, without thinking.

Wendy paused at the door, her finger prone at her inner-ear, ready to command it open.

Louise took a few seconds to collect herself. "You didn't show me where the cafeteria is."

Wendy smiled broadly, shook her head, and then said, "Get yourself washed and dressed in a clean set of overalls. The Basements aren't as big as you think they are—I'm sure you'll work out where the cafeteria is eventually." She gave a shrug. "Or else you'll starve."

With a chuckle, Wendy left the room.

Louise stood her ground, staring at the door through which Wendy had just passed.

She had no clear idea of what'd come over her; why she'd had that urge to call out to Wendy.

One thing was for certain, though, it hadn't been to ask about the cafeteria.

She'd *wanted* to ask about Njhay García.

Why that was, precisely, she couldn't fathom.

4

FIRST DAY

L ouise woke with a start.

At first she couldn't quite square what was going on . . . why those half dozen, even chimes were sounding inside her skull. Then, when she opened her eyes—her vision swamped with the watermark of the Celestial Stays Dome—she recalled where she was.

That she was on the Moon.

When her eyes came into focus, she took in the details of the programmed walls. This morning—and it was the Link which told her it *was* morning—the walls were showing off a placid, sandy beach; complete with a palm tree and sleepy, lapping waves.

She hoiked herself up and out of bed, and into the shower where she took a quick dip.

Once she was all dressed in her royal-blue overalls, and still feeling something like jetlag following the voyage a day or more earlier, she made her way through the corridors of the Basements to the cafeteria.

Just as Wendy had hinted at the day before, Louise had found the cafeteria without too much trouble. There really *wasn't* all that much in the Basements save other employees' rooms.

Louise couldn't help but think about all the hotels she'd stayed in throughout the years and that she'd never *really* thought about how the backend of those places must look . . . well, she was getting a pretty good idea right now.

The cafeteria was about as grand as it sounded, which was to say that there was a whole series of plasticky benches which reminded Louise of dinnertime at school.

And—just like dinnertime at school—there were trays, and a queue, and a succession of options behind perspiring glass, served up by a host of other Celestial Stays employees, who, quite frankly, looked as if they would rather be anywhere else than the Moon this morning.

Louise made no remark about the two scoops of scrambled egg which were served with a pair of buttered bread rolls. Neither did she utter a sound at the fierce-smelling, black ooze which passed for coffee being squirted into an instantly recyclable cup.

She decided against the sizzling strips of bacon; the greasy, white bubbles of fat amongst the charred strips putting her off not just her breakfast, but probably her lunch too.

Once sat down at a place, and making a good go of sawing through her meal, she couldn't help but notice that she seemed to be just about the only person in the cafeteria.

She glanced about, trying to see someone else.

The only *other* person she did see was sat off over in the corner of the cafeteria. Acting on impulse, and because, quite frankly, a conversation was probably just the trick to take her mind off breakfast, she ventured over with her tray, very much feeling like she was the new girl at school.

If she did feel like the new girl at school, then she was at least consoled by the fact that she recognised the other person. A fellow new recruit.

The woman who had had trouble with her Guardian the day before:

K. SINGH, as she read off the nametag.

"Hi," Louise said, beaming a smile at the woman.

The woman smiled back, her own egg breakfast sat before her, and, like Louise's, mostly untouched.

"Do you mind if I sit here?" Louise said.

"No," the woman replied. "Go ahead."

Louise sank onto the bench, setting her tray before her. When she glanced down she was somewhat disappointed that the visual hadn't improved on the way here. She had hoped that the act of burning off calories by crossing the cafeteria might've worked up sufficient hunger to negate such things as *appearance* . . . but apparently not.

"I'm Louise," Louise said, reaching her hand across the table, and then added, "British," as it seemed to be the done thing within the Celestial Stays Dome.

"Kyra," the woman replied. "*Indian.*"

"Looking forward to your first day?"

The woman—*Kyra*—forked up some scrambled egg along with the soggy bread roll. She wrinkled her nose, as if working up courage. She glanced back at Louise. "I guess so."

"Any idea why there's nobody else around?"

"From what my Guardian told me, we get an easier first day, a chance to acclimatise to the artificial gravity, to come around to the new conditions. An opportunity to get some sleep in."

"Sounds like a good idea. But where're the others?"

"Oh," Kyra replied, nodding over Louise's shoulder. "They're dribbling their way in."

Sure enough, when Louise looked around, she saw that three other new recruits were now standing with their trays at the ready, waiting to be served their breakfasts.

If only they knew . . .

"So," Louise said, lifting her fork to her lips, finally having plucked up the courage to take a mouthful, "what've you been assigned to?"

"Guided tours."

"You sound enthusiastic."

Kyra flashed a sarcastic smile, then returned to perusing her eggs.

Unlike Louise, she hadn't yet taken One Small Step for Breakfast Kind.

"I . . . well," Kyra got out. "It's complicated, okay?"

Louise chewed on her eggs, surprised that they weren't as bad as they looked; heavy on the butter, easy on the salt. She swallowed them away and then risked a sip of coffee.

After spitting the sip back into the cup, she turned again to Kyra.

"I saw you were having some trouble with your assignment yesterday, back at Entry Clearance. Is everything okay now?"

"Yeah," Kyra said, looking distracted, or else fascinated by some other member of the new recruits queuing for their breakfast. "It was just some glitch with the Link." She turned her attention back to Louise. "All fixed."

They went on eating their breakfast in silence, and Louise had to admit she was glad for it. Once she'd got through with her breakfast, she wished Kyra a good day and laid her tray down on the pile for one of the droids to collect. Next, she headed back through the corridors, to her quarters, where she brushed her teeth.

On her way back out of the Basements, she found herself in the lift with a pair of Celestial Stays employees wearing different-coloured overalls; a man and a woman.

Whereas all other employees within the Dome wore royal-blue, these two were in a deep-space black. All her life Louise had had a slight fear of authority figures; police, soldiers, and, as these obviously were, Security personnel.

Both of them, Louise saw, wore blaster pistols holstered at their thighs.

Thankfully, she noticed that the two of them had their safety switches activated.

Just as every kid down on Earth learned, it was only when the light on the blaster grip shifted away from green to orange—STUN—and then over to red—LETHAL—that there was any reason for panic. Louise caught the woman's eye, and read her nametag:

L. NIU

She recognised the flag as belonging to China.

Although Louise was convinced that she was subtle about her glance, she realised, when she pulled back, as the lift reached the surface, that the female security employee—L. NIU—was eyeballing her firmly. Louise managed the shred of a smile and a weak, "Good day" as she slipped out of the lift.

Louise was surprised at how simple it was for her to catch a PEAR to the Crescent Gardens.

As soon as she stepped in through the entrance she found herself grabbed by Wendy.

As with the day before, Wendy was grinning from ear to ear.

She whipped Louise along through the force field. Even though she had effortlessly shimmied through it yesterday, Louise couldn't help but feel a knotted dread that something might go wrong today; that the force field might—of its own volition—cut her in half.

Thankfully, it didn't.

Wendy whisked Louise through the now-familiar corridors of the Crescent Gardens building, not pausing when they passed by the laboratory, where, Louise noted, Njhay was hard at work on something or other.

She felt her stomach dip slightly.

A couple of quickened heartbeats.

Then she tried to forget she'd felt anything at all.

Wendy soon set Louise to work on some flowerbeds; or what was, apparently, the *kitchen* garden. These very fruits and vegetables, Wendy assured her, were served to the guests at the Lunar Grand . . . Louise was of half a mind to ask where the food they were served in the Basements came from, but she managed to hold herself back.

She was given a hoe and told to till the soil in neat little rows.

Wendy demonstrated the first and then stood back to see how well Louise had learned.

"Well," Wendy said, brushing the loose soil from her hands as she walked away. "Call me if you run into any trouble."

It was around midmorning, or, to be precise, at eleven-hundred hours, when Louise caught sight of Njhay across the Gardens. She mopped her brow with the back of her hand and leaned on the hoe, allowing herself some time to get her breath back. She knew how surreal this sight must appear to anybody unacquainted with the daily toil within the Celestial Stays Dome.

Here she was, tilling the soil, working the land, just as humans had done for centuries back on Earth . . . the only difference being that she was no longer *on* Earth.

She was tilling earth on the *Moon*.

Still dressed in his white lab coat, she watched on as Njhay crouched down to inspect some plant or other. She saw that he held a pair of scissors in his hand and that he was working to take clippings.

For a long few seconds, Louise found herself engrossed by Njhay's muscular hands, and she couldn't help thinking about how they might feel up against her own skin, almost as if that taste she'd had the other day, when they'd shaken hands, had just been the start . . .

She killed the fantasy.

Turned her attention to practicalities.

Back to the world—the *real* world.

She watched on as he slipped the clippings into a resealable, transparent plastic bag. She wondered how Celestial Stays viewed someone like Njhay, if it was just as laid bare as it had been the day before, when she'd personally witnessed the cool tone Angliss had treated Njhay with. Were scientists on the Moon really so reluctantly tolerated?

She wondered why she cared so much.

She had her own problems after all.

She turned away from Njhay, and focussed her attention on the task before her.

If she worked, she could keep herself from thinking.

She could prevent the past, like invisible, knotted tree roots, from tripping her up time and time again.

Now it was time for her to forget.

Now it was time for her to *escape*.

"My, oh, my, blue eyes."

On her knees, patting down soil, Louise glanced up from her work.

Caught sight of Supervisor Angliss standing over her.

Louise took in Angliss's flowing red hair. Her handsome features. And, above all else, the golden Supervisor's patch stitched to the breast pocket of her overalls.

"You *have* been busy, Louise."

And she *had* been busy.

Louise was strangely proud of the well-ordered rows of soil which she had sculpted out of the earth. Of how *pretty* it seemed that what had been just this morning a patch of soil thick with weeds was now planted with potatoes.

Perhaps this was the kind of subtlety that somebody with the obvious business nous of Angliss could never quite understand.

A hard day of physical work well done . . .

Louise felt a little more together now, it being almost the end of her first day. She had begun to feel natural in this environment, under these *unusual* conditions.

She found herself regaining a little of her former pep.

"I'm sorry," Louise replied, "I didn't realise we were on first-name terms."

This, Louise was glad to observe, served to immediately straighten out the face-splitting smile Angliss was wearing.

"Well," Angliss said, her voice deadpan now, "I don't think I ever told you *my* first name, did I?"

Louise straightened up, and then, almost losing her balance as she did so, she stood at her full height. She was a little disappointed to note that she was several centimetres shorter than Angliss.

"Mackenzie," Angliss said. "Mackenzie Angliss, from Hammondville, New South Wales. Third lunar rotation for Celestial Stays, if you please." She gave a mock curtsey and then feigned a nasal British accent. "So delighted to make your acquaintance."

Louise felt herself simmer slightly.

It was strange. She had spent such a peaceable day here, in the Crescent Gardens. And it seemed such a fragile thing that it could be easily shattered by the simplest off-hand comment.

All the same, she was determined the day *wouldn't* be ruined.

She breathed deeply.

Calmed herself down.

Told herself to see what *Mackenzie* wanted, and then wish her on her way.

She reached down for the hoe, gripped it tightly in her fist.

"I was just wondering," Mackenzie said, casting a glance about their surroundings, as if there might be someone nearby willing to spy on them, "if you might be interested in coming to a party this evening."

" 'A party' ?" Louise replied, a little taken aback. "*Why?*"

Mackenzie bulged her eyes and gave an elaborate shrugging gesture. "Does there always *need* to be a reason to have a party—can't one be *spontaneous* once in a while?"

Again, Mackenzie was affecting a British accent.

And it was really starting to get on Louise's nerves.

She squeezed the hoe tighter still.

Mackenzie continued, "I'm sure that you've heard of Costantino Zito, have you not?"

Louise, of course, had.

Costantino Zito Junior was one of the leading dealers in media broadcasting on Earth—if not *the* leader . . . Just as everybody knew the Celestial Stays jingle off-by-heart, so did they effortlessly use Zito as an interchangeable word for entertainment.

Why, when a child, Louise had asked her parents more times than she could count to 'go on the Zito for a bit'. Later, at university—*after work*—she would 'unwind with a bit of Zito'.

"Yes, well," Mackenzie continued, "*Zito* happens to be arriving next week and, as you might expect, he is looking forward to a stellar experience at the Celestial Stays Dome." She paused, bringing her fingers up to her bottom lip and tapping them there, apparently absentmindedly.

Louise couldn't help but notice that Mackenzie hadn't once gone for her earpiece for the entirety of their conversation. She wondered if this might be some sort of record.

"The party . . ." Mackenzie rolled her eyes, noting what Louise supposed to be her *reluctant* expression . . . "the *meeting*, will merely be a collection of Guardians and Supervisors, all come together to discuss cross-Division collaboration in anticipation for Señor Zito's visit."

"But I'm not a Guardian," Louise said. "And I'm certainly not a *Supervisor*."

A smile tweaked the corner of Mackenzie's mouth. "No, blue eyes," she said. "You're not; that much is true. However"—here she did pause, sticking her finger into her inner-ear, sending off an order to who-knew-where—"you *do* have some very relevant past experience." She arched an eyebrow. "Working at Humble Associates? I imagine, in the role of 'Public Relations Manager' you spent a great deal of time managing the Great and the Good, no?"

Once more, Louise got that sinking feeling; the unplaceable

sensation that she was disappearing down through the surface of the Moon. That she might keep on going until . . .

She planted the hoe into the earth, using it to steady herself.

She knew what it would mean to get involved with all this—to be *swept up* in all of these goings-on with the preparations for Costantino Zito's visit.

And she wanted no part in it.

Louise shook her head, but Mackenzie was fast.

"What're you hiding, Louise?" Mackenzie said. "Or do I need to get in touch with Humble Associates to ask them directly?"

A chill ran down Louise's spine.

Her blood froze in her veins.

Feeling the hoe slipping through her fingers, she tightened her grip. But it was no good. It was too late. The hoe slipped. It landed —with a damp, metallic *thud*—at her feet.

Louise didn't stoop to retrieve it.

When Louise spoke again, her voice was a husky whisper. "No . . . you won't have to do that."

"Good," Mackenzie said, again jabbing her finger into her inner-ear as she trod away. "I'll have Security come by to pick you up." She flashed a smile. "I wouldn't want you to get lost."

Louise watched on as Mackenzie retreated along the gravel pathway, falling behind the foliage. Finally slipping out of sight.

As Louise reached down for the hoe, now lying at her feet, she couldn't help catching sight of Njhay emerging once more from his laboratory, blinking rapidly in the bright light of the Dome.

No doubt he had come outside to get some fresh air, or to take some more clippings.

He glanced over at her, smiled, and then trudged off toward one of the flowerbeds.

What Louise wouldn't have given to be like him, to have been carefree, to be able to hide herself away in some laboratory. Away from prying eyes.

Away from *everything*.

But she had been found.

And there was nothing she could do.

5

HIDDEN

As Njhay crouched down to hide behind a clump of aloe vera, he decided there was something about Louise which he couldn't quite put his finger on.

Was it how Wendy had put her to work throughout the entire day on those kitchen allotments, and how she had—*bloody-mindedly*—stuck with it?

Even—from what he had seen of her—*enjoying* it.

At least until Supervisor Angliss had shown up.

He wondered if it was Louise's beautiful face. Those crystalline blue eyes. The blond hair which tumbled down in waves to that spot just between her shoulder blades. How she had the kind of body which was made for anything other than hard work.

And that was where his imagination began to get carried away . . .

This was his fifth rotation on Luna, and, before he'd come, he'd made up his mind that it would be his last. He was sick of trying to do his work—*important work*—with both hands tied behind his back.

How someone like Wendy—who had been going here for eight rotations—managed to find that ever elusive balance between science and *finance* escaped him. And, what was more, why she *bothered* to find the balance, escaped him further still.

People, Njhay had decided, long ago, just weren't worth the effort.

They were constantly changing.

That was what he liked about plants. How they were a constant. How they wouldn't up and change their mind in the middle of the night . . .

How they wouldn't walk away without reason or explanation.

Feeling the same anger—the same frustration; the same broken heart plaguing him—he snipped off a cutting of the aloe vera leaf, and, with far more force than was necessary, jabbed it down into the resealable plastic bag and squeezed it shut.

Look at him, taking out his pains on his plants.

Was there anything lower?

As Njhay made his way back to his lab—the only place within the Celestial Stays Dome where he could experience anything like relaxation these days—he received an incoming message through his neural implant. Even as the steady, even, gender-neutral voice of the Link read it to him, he couldn't quite get his brain around the concept.

Once more, human logic evaded him . . .

6

PREPARATION

ot quite knowing what to expect from the evening, and having been told, at least at first, that this was going to be a 'party', Louise was understandably thrown into a panic.

Standing in her room, she noted, as she had the day before, that her wardrobe was filled with nothing but the royal-blue overalls of Celestial Stays.

For the first time in her life, she could say that she had *literally* nothing to wear . . . not unless the occasion tonight was fancy dress; and the theme was 'car mechanics' . . .

Louise was taken off guard when her earpiece informed her that there was somebody at her door.

At first, as she padded across the room to go answer, she couldn't help but cast her mind back to this morning, with Kyra, at breakfast.

For some reason, Louise got it into her mind that Kyra had come to apologise for her *awkwardness* at breakfast this morning.

Then, since Louise found this to be a far-fetched notion, she decided that it must be Wendy; that *Wendy* was the strong arm Mackenzie would utilise to get her to the ball . . .

So Louise was surprised when she opened the door to find an unfamiliar woman standing there.

In fact, for the first few seconds, she was rendered stunned.

The woman was about Louise's age and had a cute, doll-like face; peach-coloured cheeks. Her brunette hair was cropped short so that it jagged down about her ears. There was something somewhat restrained about her, a sense of introversion when held up in comparison with either Wendy or Mackenzie. She held back from the doorway almost as if she was embarrassed.

"Hi," Louise finally got out.

The woman smiled back at her, showing off neat rows of white teeth. "Hi."

Only now did Louise notice the black plastic bag which the woman held dangling from one of her hands. Strange that she would've overlooked it, but—*she supposed*—the shock of finding an unfamiliar woman at her door had thrown her somewhat.

The woman blushed slightly. "I'm Alicia," she said, in what Louise took to be a North-American accent. A glance to the Stars and Stripes sewn on beside the silver Guardian badge on her overalls confirmed Louise's suspicions.

"Wood Dale, Illinois," the woman—*Alicia*—jabbered out.

With a quick blink, bringing her manners back into focus, Louise replied, "Bristol, UK."

There was a brief pause and then Alicia, apparently absorbing the awkwardness, shook the bag she held, making the plastic crackle. "Got word that you might need some threads for tonight."

"Oh, thanks," Louise said, eyeing the plastic bag differently now. She reached for it.

Alicia didn't hand the bag over. "I was, uh, wondering," she continued, "when Mackenzie came to me, when she said that you needed a little *help*, that you might need some other . . . *supplies?*"

Alicia transferred the plastic bag to her other hand, revealing that she also had a black box.

"What's in there?" Louise said.

"Oh, you'll see."

———

Alicia's secret box contained makeup.

Lots of makeup.

And since Alicia deemed the static bathroom mirror unfit for purpose, she showed Louise which program she needed to dial up on her wallpaper to turn the entire bedroom into a walk-in mirror.

And so, sat on a chair in the middle of the mirrors, Louise allowed Alicia to tend to her hair and makeup, bringing her blond hair up into an elegant bunch at the top of her head, and then bringing it down in layers.

Louise hadn't had her hair done since . . . well, since she'd worked for Humble Associates.

They were so busy chatting away about life under the Celestial Stays Dome that Louise didn't think to ask Alicia anything about herself till the hair-and-makeup job was all but finished.

As Louise took in the creamy tones of the eyeshadow she now wore, and the blusher spread across her cheeks, and how it accentuated the blueness of her eyes—or turned them into glimmering 'sapphires', as Alicia put it—she decided to right this wrong.

"So," Louise said, "I suppose you work in Hospitality, helping to get guests ready for all the big occasions? All those famous penthouse parties at the Lunar Grand?"

Alicia shook her head. "Nope, they've got their own designers and seamstresses working over there." Standing behind Louise as she sat in the chair, Alicia met her eye in the mirror, bringing her hands up to the side of Louise's face, correcting a couple of misplaced curls. "Whenever there's an emergency among the employees, I'm the one they call."

"What do you do, then?"

"I don't suppose you've heard of the Orbital Café?"

Louise grinned. "Don't be modest—you work there?"

"Actually," Alicia replied, combing along one of the layers she'd put in, "I run the place. Catering, that's my Division."

Louise found herself knocked back for several seconds. "You *run* the Orbital Café?"

The next words Louise wanted to blurt out were, *But you're so young!*

She held herself back, though.

When she'd worked for Humble Associates, there'd been nothing more annoying than having that fact thrown in her face.

"Yep," Alicia said, with a slight shrug, but with an unmissable —*if subtle*—smile of pride.

Louise allowed herself to slouch back slightly. She stared into the mirror, at Alicia's reflection as she stood behind her, making the last minute tweaks to her appearance.

Only now did Louise fully realise that Alicia's eyes were neither brown or green; that they were a kind of tangerine colour. Gorgeous. She couldn't help wondering why a beautiful girl such as she would take herself so far away from Earth.

Away from so many eligible bachelors . . . just as Louise had done.

"All-righty," Alicia said, taking a step back from Louise, in the same manner an artist might give themselves room to take in a canvas—to give their latest artwork a touch of distance. Apparently satisfied, she switched her attention onto Louise's face. "Wanna see the dress?"

In all the fuss over her hair and makeup, Louise had almost forgotten about the dress.

Almost . . . but not quite.

Alicia rightly made something of a show unzipping the bag and slowly—*ever so slowly*—slipping the dress out from within.

For several seconds, Louise was rendered stunned by the sight; her eyes caught up in the flowing, reflective material. It was strapless and she could tell that the hem would come down to about her middle thigh.

This was certainly not just *any* dress.

As Alicia approached her, Louise noted another aspect of the dress; that it was transparent.

This threw her for a moment until Alicia—apparently reading the concern in her face—pressed on a smile and said, "The dress works to compliment your natural hair and skin tone. Don't worry, we'll allow it to flesh out a bit before you leave the room."

Louise rose up out of the chair, breathing in a little of the strong, lilac perfume which Alicia had enthusiastically squirted over her. Alicia helped her into the dress. She zipped it up.

Alicia had been telling the truth, because, no sooner had the zip been brought up to the nape of Louise's neck, than the dress began to swirl; to blur Louise's naked skin beneath.

To transform it into the colour of clotted cream.

It remained that shade for a matter of moments before taking on a subtle green shade.

Whenever Louise attempted to pin down the colour to any one definition, looking herself over in the mirror, she came up short.

When she turned to Alicia, Alicia reached out and—*gently*—gripped Louise's chin.

She pushed Louise's latched-open jaw shut.

"There," Alicia said. "Much better."

Slowly feeling her senses returning to her, Louise turned to Alicia, looked away from the dress. "I mean," Louise said, "I've seen variable fabrics before, but, well, it's more to do with how it all hangs together so nicely. You must've been a designer in a former life."

Alicia blushed a touch. "Something like that," she said.

Although Louise would've liked to follow up on this little morsel, she was disturbed by another notification from the Link that there was somebody else at the door.

Seeing that Louise had turned her head, Alicia said, "That must be your armed escort." She narrowed her eyes in a playful fashion. "You know, you've either done something to really impress Mackenzie." She paused. "Or to *really* piss her off."

"Which is better?" Louise said, padding across the room to answer the door.

"I wouldn't like to say."

7

INVITED PARTICIPATION

Louise recognised her escort to the party-cum-meeting.

It was the same member of the security team she'd run into in the lift a day earlier.

The severe-looking woman who had the nametag: L. NIU.

Although it was akin to bleeding a pebble, she managed to establish that the woman's first name was Lan, and that she was from Shanghai, China. She seemed to be about the same age as Louise, but that was where the similarities appeared to end.

As the two of them sat silently in the PEAR, spindling through the air, making a beeline for the Lunar Grand, Louise took in Lan's prim, jet-black hair.

She had tucked it into a complicated sequence of plaits, and Louise decided that Lan's hair was probably long enough to extend most of the distance down her back.

When Lan let her hair down—*if she ever did*—it would be quite a sight.

The PEAR arrived on the landing strip of the Lunar Grand, and

Louise stepped out over the side. She glanced back to Lan with the intention of thanking her for her company, but the PEAR's visor was already winding its way back down, and—faster than Louise had time to blink—the PEAR whipped back up into the air and away.

Louise turned her attention to the entrance of the Lunar Grand.

She stared long and hard at the brass fixings on the doors.

And the slickly polished floors.

Her reflection seemed to crop up on every side.

She'd thought that she'd left all this behind.

Apparently not.

———

Thanks to the kind indications of one of the members of the Hospitality staff within the Lunar Grand, she knew to take the lift up to the twenty-seventh floor. From there it was a simple matter of following the throbbing bassline . . . now she saw what Mackenzie had meant by this being more of a 'party' than a meeting . . .

And, still, Louise was somewhat in the dark over just why her presence here was required at all.

A red, velvet curtain marked the entrance to the venue. Louise took a deep breath, glanced about her, as if she might be able to find some way out of this.

Seeing no other option, she sashayed in around the curtain.

She instantly felt the body heat—that reassuring, human glow.

The room was rendered in a half-light, with a strobe flickering artificial lightning every few seconds. It brought the gyrating bodies on the dance floor into stark, full-day contrast for a fraction of a second before surrendering to darkness again.

The effect was somewhat disorientating.

Back at Humble, though, Louise had done business in far more lurid places.

Not seeing where she should go next, she eyed the bar and made for it. She hadn't so much as located the barman before she heard a familiar voice in her ear.

"Made it, then, blue eyes?"

Louise turned, took in Mackenzie standing beside her. She looked to her hands, and saw that she held a glass of something. Since no intoxicating beverages or substances were officially permitted on the Moon, Louise supposed that it was some sort of carbonated fruit juice. Mackenzie herself was wearing a single-strap, scarlet-red dress which shimmied down her elegant body. Her red hair had been drawn up into a ragged bunch at the back of her head, reminding Louise, in some way, of the orchids she'd passed by in the Crescent Gardens.

There was no sign of her golden Supervisor's badge.

Not tonight.

"Come on," Mackenzie said, grabbing hold of Louise's wrist and guiding her across the packed dance floor.

Louise had to admit she was glad not to be pushed into dancing. Truth be told—following her toil in the Crescent Gardens that day—she was feeling a little stiff in the legs. She imagined that—if she did try some dancing—she'd carry it off with all the grace of a dry twig.

"Over here!" Mackenzie shouted over the music.

Why she bothered to say anything at all escaped Louise. Once Mackenzie had caught her in her death grip, she'd given not one suggestion that she would let go.

Mackenzie eased herself down onto a circular sofa which surrounded a table. There were maybe a dozen or so people packed all around. It was impossible to identify faces except when the strobe light brought them into a stark, split-second-long contrast.

Before Louise could full appreciate those she was meeting with, Mackenzie spoke into her ear again. "How does it feel to be sat at the Supervisor's table?!"

"Huh?!" Louise replied, but she had heard just fine.

Slowly, she took in the faces, those sitting around her.

And although she didn't recognise their features yet by heart, she knew that, in the coming days and weeks, they would come to dominate her thoughts.

The Supervisors of Hospitality, Catering, Tourism, Security and, of course—*Mackenzie*—Human Resources.

She took in the men and women sat there, all of them, without exception several years older than Mackenzie was.

Louise couldn't help turning her mind back to that conversation she'd had with Njhay, when he'd suggested that Mackenzie saw her as a threat.

Was this some kind of wild intimidation tactic?

It would run along the same lines of how Mackenzie had got Louise to come here in the first place; how she had threatened to ruin Louise's future with her past.

She couldn't help but cast a glance around her. Searching for an exit. A habit she had acquired. But, as she well knew, it was one thing to locate an exit; quite another to know where to run to . . .

Louise wasn't quite sure how the Supervisors managed to get any business done at the side of the dance floor, with the throbbing music, and the overwhelming body heat.

But they all seemed to be chatting along quite happily.

She wondered if some of the older Supervisors had families back home—on Earth—and if they took these eighteen-month contracts up on Luna as a 'well-earned', extended vacation; not just from their day-to-day routine, but from their wedding vows.

Loyalty, Louise had learned—in business and in life—was a matter of personal opinion.

"Louise?"

Again, it was a familiar voice, but, this time, not Mackenzie . . . if it *had* been Mackenzie, Louise had no doubt that it would've been accompanied by some intrusive gesture; a grab of her wrist, shoulder or elbow. And there was no bodily contact at all.

When she did turn to look, she was taken aback.

A new arrival.

He had just taken his place beside her on the sofa.

Njhay.

To say he was the last person she'd expected to see here—in the Lunar Grand, in the belly of the *business* beast—was an understatement. She couldn't help noticing that he hadn't scrubbed up badly at all.

Tonight, in keeping with the formal dress of the other attendees, he wore a well-cut, nice-fitting tuxedo. He didn't wear his glasses and—from the way he was squinting in the near-darkness of the room—she supposed he wasn't wearing contact lenses either.

When she breathed in, she caught the scent of honey, and she couldn't help wondering if this might be the result of some invention of his in the Crescent Gardens laboratory. He'd tamed his hair, too, as far as it would *be* tamed . . . which was to say that there seemed to be a certain logic to how the wild tufts stood up off his scalp.

"Want to get some air?!" he bellowed over the music.

Louise nodded that she did.

She glanced back to Mackenzie, expecting to find herself on the end of that laser beam-like, emerald-green stare. Pulling her back down onto the sofa; unwilling to allow her to go anywhere of her own volition, where she might slip out of sight and get up to, well, just about *anything*.

Njhay led the way through the bodies on the dance floor.

Several times, Louise had the urge to reach out and take hold of the hand he allowed to trail so casually down at his side. But she held herself back. She couldn't make the jump. She *knew* just what it would mean ... and she just wasn't *ready*.

She felt cool air coming from somewhere. A moment or so later, as she navigated a pair of entwined dancers, they emerged onto a balcony.

It looked out across the entirety of the Dome.

Louise was so struck by the sight that she almost kept on walking, right over the edge. If it hadn't been for Njhay's muscular arm reaching across her abdomen, blocking her progress, she wondered if she might've just kept on going.

Taking a fatal tumble.

It took her heart a couple of seconds to catch up with her brain. When it did, she felt it skip about in her chest, knocking against her ribs.

Njhay continued to hold her, as if she might be of a mind to go jumping.

A moment or so later, he released his hold, smiled. "You really don't want to check yourself into the Infirmary," he said. "Most of these doctors are used to dealing with minor cosmetic procedures; I'm not all that sure if they'd be all that competent at handling broken bones."

Louise breathed in deeply, consciously allowing her shoulders to go slack. She stared out over the entirety of the Celestial Stays Dome; to the Stellar Tide Casino alongside the Lunar Grand, and then to the wavy structure of the Armstrong Archive . . . she could just about make out the Orbital Café alongside it; the establishment which Alicia was responsible for.

Everything was illuminated with dazzling, white lights.

It reminded Louise of some sort of fairyland . . . a flight of fancy.

Then again, she did suppose this was the Moon.

She almost missed the Crescent Gardens, only later realising that they were vaguely illuminated with a couple of those same white lights; here and there.

Something within her pined to be back.

To be back among the plants.

Closer to the soil.

Funny to think that now she'd travelled so far away from Earth, she craved to return. Or perhaps it was just that urge which made her human. That unshakable connection to Earth—*her home.*

She turned back to Njhay, standing calmly beside her.

It was almost as if they had left a storm behind them, the clattering caterwaul of the music from the dance floor continued to bleed out into the night air. It was incredible to believe that people would travel so far—*that they would come all this way*—just to seal themselves indoors.

Away from what was outside.

Away from the Moon.

She looked over Njhay's bronze-green eyes, then found herself saying, "Why're you here? You don't fit."

To begin with, she thought Njhay would dismiss this comment with some throwaway smile, or some snippy remark.

Instead, though, he stared back at her, into her own eyes, then said, "I know." He breathed in deeply, that honey scent of his wafting over Louise, and added, "I have a proposal—well, that is to say, I was called upon here. I was *required.*"

Louise frowned. "What for?"

"You'll see."

This time he did smile, and he stared out across the lunar landscape.

His mind could've been on just about anything at all.

They must've been standing on the balcony for about five minutes when Louise received a notification from Mackenzie, wanting to know where she was.

When she shifted her gaze onto Njhay, she saw that he had received a similar message.

They both wore the same smile.

Before she was quite aware of what was happening, she felt her whole body moving into his. Her lips inevitably moving toward his. She wasn't sure if it was an extra *throb* of the bassline which made her jump the gap, all she knew was that she was the one who closed the final distance.

Her lips pressed up against his.

And her hand reached out, coming to rest on his firm, muscular chest.

It felt as if an hour passed with the two of them holding the pose.

And then Louise heard the notification of another message arriving.

Another message from Mackenzie.

When she pulled away from Njhay, she felt as if she was floating. As if her feet would never again find their way back to the ground. She wondered if the artificial Dome gravity had hit a blip, but then she felt the tightening sensation in her chest; that same sense of panic returning.

Her stomach dropped.

She couldn't do this again.

Not *again*.

Although Njhay smiled easily at her, she couldn't find it within herself to respond in kind.

And, before she said anything further, before he could kiss her again, she was gone.

8

COOPERATION

Njhay watched her leaving him. He watched on as she slipped back into the Lunar Grand. He had been thinking about that kiss all day; had been wondering if it would truly come to pass. They had only just met, and yet, look at him. He was supposed to have made up his mind; he was *supposed* to have decided that he was going to leave the Moon following this rotation; that he would find somewhere to carry out his work Earthside.

Now wasn't the time for attachments.

Then again, what about a kiss suggested an *attachment*?

Hadn't he made a promise to himself—*long ago*—that he wouldn't get close again?

That he wouldn't risk having his heart broken?

He had told himself that he would greet the world with a stoic, cold exterior; that he would discourage any kind of positive social interaction.

Sex, yes, there was that; but, as he well knew—as all men were *supposed* to know—it was so easily divorced from tenderness, from kindness . . . from *love*.

Was that what he felt now, for Louise?

He couldn't quite fathom it.

Couldn't quite understand how he'd *allowed* this to happen.

Another message arrived in his inner-ear from Mackenzie, scolding him to get on with it. For him to return to their 'meeting'. God, how he hated all of these pseudo-social events; it would've much better suited him to meet with the Supervisors just after eight-hundred hours in some stuffy meeting room over a cup of coffee. But, no, he'd had to go and get himself all dolled-up . . . and that'd affected his brain, made him curious about Louise; anxious to bring her close to him.

He arched his shoulders, working a crick out of his lower back, and then stepped inside.

The music had boiled down substantially, so much so that he could make out voices over the top of the bassline now. He saw that Mackenzie headed up the other Supervisors, and that she was keeping them entertained in that *way* she had of doing.

He drew in a breath and repressed the urge to sigh it straight back out.

No, he needed to at least *appear* proud, even if pride had long ago deserted him.

Even if he'd long ago shed his role of scientist to take on the lesser mantel of Cheap Purveyor of Party Tricks . . . if only his parents could see him now; if only his *grandfather* could see him now.

All that time invested—*all that money spent*—so he might do something like this.

Mackenzie turned away from the rest of the Supervisors.

She dealt him a frosty glare.

Then turned up the corners of her mouth with her best professional smile.

This was it. His time to shine. Or something like that . . .

He withdrew the transparent, resealable plastic bag from his tuxedo pocket.

Within, he had a cutting from the aloe vera plant he had cowered behind earlier that day.

He trod toward the group of Supervisors, feeling their eyes upon him.

When he felt himself a decorous distance away, he undid the plastic bag, removing the cut-off piece of aloe vera plant from within.

It amused him to see those expressions all fixed on the cutting.

He wondered how many times the Supervisors had mocked him and other scientists—*historians, and the like*—for their 'unprofitable' work . . . well, now he hoped to turn the tables on them.

He was about to show them something which might turn out to be Very Profitable Indeed.

He crouched down and then set the cutting on the dance floor.

All eyes remained glued to the plant.

Waiting for something to happen.

Expecting something to happen.

He noted Mackenzie's concerned sidelong glance.

And it made him glad.

He was *glad* that she felt discomfort . . . that *she* might end up being humiliated.

For a long few seconds, he considered flunking the demonstration, pretending that something had gone irretrievably wrong. That would infuriate Mackenzie. It would turn her into a ball of hate. And there was no telling what the consequences for him might personally be; but, then again, hadn't he made up his mind to leave the Celestial Stays Dome behind forever?

In the end, though, he still possessed his pride.

And, what was more, he knew that, as long as he lived, he would die to protect it.

With the Supervisors beginning to mumble amongst themselves, Njhay triggered the program through his neural transmitter. And then there was nothing to do but stand back to watch.

There were another few uncomfortable moments as the Supervisors remained focussed on the cutting of aloe vera plant, and then, as if by magic—*as if science wasn't involved at all*—it began to glow with a milky-white light.

Somebody had knocked the music down another couple of notches in volume, because Njhay clearly heard a collective gasp escape the assembled Supervisors.

The tiny piece of aloe vera plant continued to glow brightly. When it reached a crescendo, it faded—*like a twinkling star in the sky*—before brightening once again.

Knowing he had their attention, Njhay explained.

"The entirety of the Crescent Gardens are pumped with the stuff—it's all ready to be activated when our distinguished guest arrives."

He couldn't quite bring himself to utter the name of a chancer like Costantino Zito out loud.

There was a smattering of applause from the Supervisors, and lots of satisfied smiles. When the noise died down, and with the music still thrumming away in the background—an unkillable weed—one of the Supervisors spoke up. "Does it damage the plants?"

Njhay shook his head. "No, the compound is entirely benevolent. In fact," he went on, "it will expire within the course of a fort-night; rendered ordinary, everyday tap water."

"There's still something of a miracle about even tap water on the Moon," the Supervisor of Tourism—Refilwe Mbemba—put in.

Njhay smiled along with the pleasant chuckles. He could tell that the Supervisors hadn't been entirely compliant with the 'NO INTOXICATING SUBSTANCES' rule . . . then again, they were the ones who made the rules; at least on Luna.

Finally, Mackenzie broke from the group, still smiling away, as if she had just experienced the most 'charming' little trinket . . . little did she know how much pain—how many chemical burns—Njhay had had to go through in order to achieve this effect. And how much toil it'd taken to dose the entirety of the Gardens with the stuff.

"Excellent, quite frankly," Mackenzie said, her back to Njhay now. "I should think that Señor Zito will be nothing but enchanted."

The Supervisors applauded again and then returned to their drinks.

Njhay noticed the volume of the music crank up a couple of notches.

Mackenzie glanced about the room, and then turned into him. "You don't happen to know where Louise has got to, do you?"

Njhay looked around.

Funny, he had almost forgotten about her; but now that Mackenzie had brought her back up, he felt an odd twinge at the base of his gut. Had she got under his skin so easily?

Remembering that he still needed to reply, Njhay said, "I think I overheard her telling someone she had a headache, that she was going to go lie down." He shrugged, as if this would help to show how nonchalant he was when all the time his heart was beating its way up his throat. "She only got here yesterday, I imagine she's still suffering from the effects."

Mackenzie pouted, and then breathed in deeply, as if she was readying to launch into a tirade.

Njhay was in no doubt that she'd registered the hesitation throughout his display; that he'd toyed with the idea of humiliating her . . . but, as it was, he *had* put on the display—a *successful* display —and so, as it stood, there was nothing she could do.

"It would have been nice to see her," Mackenzie said. "She would probably have had some valuable ideas on how to treat our special guest."

"How so?" Njhay found himself replying.

Mackenzie caught him with the corner of her eye. "Oh," she said, with a thin-lipped smile. "Just her past experience—what she used to do back down on Earth."

"What *did* she used to do back down on Earth?"

As soon as the words slipped past his lips, he cursed himself for so obviously showing his hand.

Indeed, he noted the narrowing of Mackenzie's eyes—surely she was onto him.

Onto just how he *felt* about Louise.

Apparently having caught him in her trap now, Mackenzie merely reached up and tapped the side of her nose. As she sauntered away, she even threw in a sly wink for good measure.

Njhay stood there, on the dance floor, the music grinding on around him.

Unable to stop thinking about Louise.

And that kiss.

9

ORGANIC MAINTENANCE

here was a strange calmness which descended over Louise as she worked through the flowerbeds, raking up dead leaves and flower petals. She picked them up with her gloved hands and deposited them in the nearby droid; the one which accompanied her throughout her duties in the Crescent Gardens.

She had nicknamed the droid 'Arnold', only for the reason that her first pet—*a mongrel Labrador-collie cross*—had been called Arnold. Something about the name sent a nostalgic fire burning in her gut; making her feel closer to home.

Helping her realise that—for the next eighteen months—this *was* her home.

Perspiration lining her forehead, she reached up and wiped it off, looking out through the Dome at the Earth set in the sky. She'd read the description given in so many of her teachings, back at school; in so many of the interviews with those who'd travelled to space, and she couldn't help but think of it as they had described it; just a tiny blue marble lying on a black velvet cloth.

So insignificant—*and yet*—so beautiful.

It was hard to believe so much could come to pass on such a tiny scrap of the universe. It was hard to believe so much could've happened to *her* in such a tiny place. But then, she supposed, when it came down to it, she was just as tiny as everything else.

Many—*many*—times tinier than the Earth itself.

As Louise straightened up, throwing off a handful of leaves into the droid's receptacle, she got the feeling that she was being watched. Indeed, when she glanced up, she saw that it was Wendy.

Louise cast off the diminutive thoughts.

As with all other Celestial Stays employees, Wendy wore the royal-blue overalls.

The Guardian's badge sewn onto her breast pocket.

"How're you getting on here?" Wendy said, casting a close eye over Louise's morning of work.

Louise gave her a gentle smile in return. "Fine," she said, dusting the earth off her gardening gloves. "I think I've got most of this licked."

Wendy glanced about, then pointed down, at the toe of Louise's boot. "Think you missed a spot."

Sure enough, when Louise looked down, she saw that a rogue leaf had stuck to her boot. She bent down, peeled it off then deposited it in the droid's receptacle.

"Well," Wendy went on, now that the rogue leaf had safely been condemned to refuse, "if our friend Costantino doesn't have himself a good time then it won't be for lack of cleanliness in the Crescent Gardens."

Strangely, Louise felt a touch of pride blossom through her chest.

'Strange', because it was odd to feel pride about a job as basic and relaxed as the one she'd done. She'd had droids to help her out. Then again, she supposed she'd begun to get used to the concept of 'work' here beneath the Celestial Stays Dome, it *had* been a week, after all.

"So," Wendy said, in a casual manner which suggested she was about to open a can of worms. "What did you used to do Earthside?"

Louise's whole body stiffened. Suddenly the sweet, homey smells of the gardens surrounding her became a poisonous mist. And she had the urge to run.

Again.

When she turned back to look at Wendy, she saw that her brow was furrowed. How could Wendy *not* have noticed Louise's reaction? She'd hardly been subtle.

Louise turned her attention down, onto the flowerbeds, and finally answered. "I used to work for a big company . . . I was a . . . uh . . . *high up* . . . fairly."

For some reason, Louise managed to half convince herself that this would be enough to sate Wendy's thirst. But of course Wendy stood firm, a slight smile on her lips, waiting for elaboration.

Louise reached out and plucked a stray dead leaf lying atop a nearby bush. She deposited it into the droid, and half hoped that Wendy would've disappeared by now.

No such luck.

Louise recalled Mackenzie's not-so subtle threats, and knew that if she failed to deliver satisfactorily with her explanation to Wendy then it was quite likely Mackenzie *would* dig down further.

If there was one thing which Louise had learned about business, and those who had a competitive nature, it was that they would be simply *ruthless* when they fixed their minds on something they wanted. They would stop at nothing to achieve their goals.

Wasn't that one of the reasons Louise had run off?

She glanced back at Wendy. "Humble Associates," she got out. "That was who I worked for."

Wendy pouted. " 'Humble Associates'," she uttered back. "And who're they when they're at home?"

Louise felt a lump form in her throat. She swallowed it back. Although Humble Associates were a fairly well-known name throughout the world of international business, it wasn't impossible somebody wouldn't have heard of them; the *umbrella* organisation of so many.

Louise breathed in deeply, preparing herself; knowing that she had talked herself into a corner now. And there would be no escape. "Humble Hardware?"

Nothing from Wendy.

"Humble Bathrooms?"

"That's the problem with spending half your life on the Moon. I suppose, you miss out on certain things—I'm sure these are all *well-respected* businesses."

Beginning to feel exasperated, both at the subject of the conversation, and at being unable to strike one of Wendy's bells, Louise had another go. "One of the brands you might recognise is Humble Greetings."

This time Wendy's face brightened slightly. She tilted her head to one side. "Yes," she replied. "*Of course.*" Her smile twisted into something approaching a sneer. "My ex-husband, he sent me one of those 'personalised' virtual greetings for our tenth wedding anniversary, the day of which, consequently, took place while he was on an *unmissable* business trip in São Paulo, Brazil. Despite me making the effort to be Earthside for such a special occasion."

She arched an eyebrow.

"Perhaps, when he took the photo that went with the greeting, he should've thought to check for lacy underwear lying on the bed. Still"—she shrugged—"it could've been worse. We could've gone *another* ten years living a lie . . . me up on the Moon; *him* with a dame in every port." She crossed her arms over her chest. "We're both much happier now, I bet."

Louise found the weight lightening from her shoulders. She was glad that Wendy had managed to divert attention away from Louise's past and onto her own.

So glad that she almost forgot to express interest.

Louise took her chance, pressing on a smile. "And what do you make of the men on the Moon?"

"Oh"—Wendy batted a hand—"*really*, I'm not interested in any of that; not anymore."

"I don't believe you."

Wendy smiled back, thick and wide, and with plenty of enamel. "Nowadays I take more pleasure in *observing* the young bucks and the impressionable does doing the courting." She paused. "And don't think I haven't noticed Njhay's attention's slipped this past week. He takes extended coffee breaks—*coffee breaks* which happen, more often than not, to conveniently intersect with what-ever your current location happens to be."

Here Louise felt herself begin to blush. All of a sudden she couldn't help wondering if she wouldn't have felt more comfort-able speaking about her past than about her *present* love life . . .

Anyway, although it was true that she and Njhay had kissed that night, a week ago, they had hardly seen one another this past week. Louise had only caught sight of Njhay on the odd occasion when he 'happened' to be walking through the Gardens; whether or not there was any ulterior motive to these walks, she couldn't

71

say. *She* wasn't privy to Njhay's thoughts. As far as she knew, the kiss had simply been an impulsive gesture; one swiftly regretted and soon forgotten.

At least for Njhay . . .

"So," Wendy went on, "any romantic plans for this evening—for Zito's arrival?"

Louise blushed some more. "I don't think there'll be time for any 'plans'."

Wendy held a finger up, then smiled broadly. "Spoken like a true Celestial Stays veteran; really, I can't quite imagine where they find you recruits; whatever the recruiters are getting paid, they should get double."

Louise felt the tension in her chest loosening as Wendy took a pair of steps away from her, apparently done with this conversation for the time being.

"Speaking of distinguished guests," Wendy continued, "there're approximately seventeen billion things that I'm supposed to be doing right now. And none of them concern digging into other people's dirty laundry—*unfortunately*," she added, with genuine disappointment.

Right as Louise thought she'd got away from the conversation unscathed, Wendy turned on her heel. Harnessed her with an intense gaze. "You probably think you're a real smart button, managing to throw me off course, trying not to spill the goods of just what *naughtiness* you got up to Earthside. But let me tell you, when it comes to gossip, and secrets, I'm second to none when it comes to sniffing them out."

Although Wendy gave a light-hearted chuckle as she turned away, clearly seeing this all as good-natured 'girl fun', Louise could only force herself to give a polite smile.

Once it was clear Wendy had slipped from visual range, she took on a far more sombre expression.

If she could only have a sense of humour about her past.

The problem was that the past was still an open wound.

Sore.

Exposed.

And—at any moment—in danger of being reopened.

10

VIP PROTOCOL

From the conversations Louise had had with fellow Celestial Stays employees, she knew that when a VIP showed up there was a very definite routine to be followed. It went without saying that the entire Dome was to be rendered spotless, since there was no telling where Mister or Missus VIP would wish to wander, and that was a part of the task with which Louise had been involved this morning in the Crescent Gardens.

With all the bustling activity which surrounded her, Louise felt impotent. She hadn't Clue One what was personally required of her so that she might contribute to the preparations.

In the end, because she couldn't think of anything else, she found herself wandering through the laboratory building of the Crescent Gardens, where she came across Njhay.

It surprised her to see that he wasn't wearing his white lab coat, and that he was comparably underdressed in only his royal-blue Celestial Stays overalls. He seemed stressed, too, his hair all standing up in tufts, and his glasses lying, forgotten, on one of the metal examination tables.

As Louise trod into the room, she breathed in that masculine scent once more—the one about which, if someone had asked her frankly a month or more ago, she would've been sure to say if she never smelled it again in all her life she would have died contented.

Now, though, it was different.

In fact, it sent a thrill through her gut.

Had it simply been a matter of leaving the planet behind?

Was that all that had been required to reconnect with her inner woman?

So that she might find herself attracted to another man?

Njhay flipped a quick glance up at her, did a double take, and then straightened himself up properly. "Oh," he said, smiling awkwardly, then added, "*Hi.*"

" 'Hi' yourself," Louise shot back, taking a few steps into the lab. "I've been wandering about the place trying to establish just what the hell I'm supposed to be doing. You haven't got any jobs for me, have you?"

"Uh," Njhay said, his mouth slightly latched open, and, Louise could see, the space behind his eyes attempting—*and failing*—to process a million things a second.

She glanced to the sink. There was a whole host of test tubes, beakers, and assorted 'scientific' paraphernalia that—to her anal-retentive eye—could do with a Good, Old-Fashioned Clean.

Before Njhay could so much as utter a sound, she sauntered past him, rolling up the sleeves of her overalls. As she drew close to him she breathed in that innately masculine, musky scent. It was so intoxicating for her that it seemed almost a pity to exhale.

But breathing, she supposed, was preferable to dying.

She slipped on a pair of rubber gloves and flipped on the hot tap.

"Uh," Njhay said, from behind her back, finally breaking his silence. "There're droids to do the cleaning, you know . . . you can leave all that for later, if—"

Louise flicked her head around, looking Njhay in those hand-some, impossibly profound bronze-green eyes of his. How many times, over these past weeks had she found herself, in idle moments, thinking about *those* eyes?

"I don't see any droids here," she replied, and then nodded to the many open cabinets. "And those cupboards are looking pretty bare of apparatus." Feeling a rush of confidence, she smiled wickedly. "And I can just tell that you're a man who *can't stand* the prospect of cross-contamination . . . I wouldn't want any of your experiments to fail just because you didn't have anybody to clean up after you."

Njhay's smile disappeared and frown lines creased his fore-head. "I . . uh . . . sorry, I'm a bit . . ."

Louise turned back to the sink, and the now-gushing hot tap. She waved a gloved hand up in the air carelessly. "Go on," she said. "Go and do whatever it is that needs doing—I'll hold the fort here. Won't break anything. *Promise.*"

For the longest time, standing at the sink, feeling the warm water through the rubber texture of her gloves, she found herself fantasising about Njhay coming up behind her, laying his muscu-lar, careful hands on her upper arms . . . and then spinning her around with an easy, powerful flick . . . pressing his lips to hers . . .

But, instead, all she heard was a slight shuffle of shoes to the door, and then, a "Thank you for this," before the sound of footfall in the corridor outside.

Louise's smile widened.

This really *was* shaping up to be a special welcome for Costantino Zito.

———————

Louise supposed she'd been washing up lab equipment for the best part of an hour, lying all the chemical-stinking glass and metal down on the sideboard so that it might drip dry.

Finally, she heard footsteps outside.

Working quickly, she shook off the final drops on the current beaker she was washing.

She rested it on the sideboard to dry.

She peeled off the gloves, hung them off the side of the sink, and then pressed on that 'wicked' smile which'd made Njhay so uncomfortable before.

She was surprised to see that it wasn't Njhay standing in the doorway, but Mackenzie.

Her whole body froze up.

The 'wicked' smile she'd been wearing previously turned to a look of horror.

"Pleased to see me, blue eyes?"

Louise caught herself before she made this situation any more awkward.

She pinned on her very best fake smile.

"I . . . thought it was someone else."

Mackenzie flashed her eyebrows. "Oh, *really?*"

Louise waited for Mackenzie to make some knowing quip, in the same manner in which Wendy had spoken; to drop an extremely strong hint that she knew all about the blossoming *thing* between Louise and Njhay.

But she added nothing else.

Nothing about *Njhay*, in any case.

"At the meeting last week, I didn't get the opportunity to properly present you to the other Supervisors. You rushed off before I got a chance to do so." Mackenzie gave a mock gasp and held her hand up to her parted lips. "You didn't try the shellfish, did you? Really, Wendy would've been able to educate you on the perils of consuming anything other than *fresh* seafood."

Knowing that there was nothing she could say to explain away her fleeing the meeting last week, she just stood there and allowed Mackenzie to have her snarky way with her.

Mackenzie drew back her thick-lipped smile, apparently done with the fun portion for the time being. "All right, then, blue eyes," she said. "To business."

Louise glanced about the lab, noting how clean she had left everything. It was strange, back on Earth, she had had maids to do just about everything; cleaning had been nothing but a waste of time. Now, though, it felt almost as if it'd been some sort of therapeutic release.

She liked to see everything in its right place.

Mackenzie went on, "During the last week, I've been in touch with Señor Zito's PA." She paused for a long moment, eyed Louise. "I happened to throw in your name, you know how it is, just trying to see if anything sticks; his PA intimated that Señor Zito would be very interested in personally meeting you . . . personally meeting somebody involved with Humble Associates."

Mackenzie might as well have punched her in the gut.

Louise reached behind her, for the edge of the sink.

Steadied herself.

Mackenzie's green eyes might as well have been a pair of heat lamps; they certainly caused Louise to sweat just as much. Finally, she regained her composure.

She regained control of her *tongue*.

"Why," Louise said, her voice frosty; huskier than she'd intended. "Why would you *do* that? Why would you mention my name?"

Mackenzie pulled a pert-lipped, ditsy expression and shrugged her shoulders. "Oh, I don't know, I suppose I wanted to cover all the bases—try to *engage* with our VIP." Her expression of feigned ditziness gave way to a more hardened look. "You do realise that Celestial Stays is a business, don't you? And, as such, we live and die by our clients—by our *guests*."

Louise opened her mouth to say something else, but Mackenzie cut her right off by holding up her palm . . . a palm which would've been wonderfully adept at stopping traffic any place, any time.

"You do realise that when you signed on to be an employee of Celestial Stays, you also bound yourself to Celestial Stays's mission statement; to our Customer Care Policy? Our *commitment* to providing the very best experience to our guests?"

Of course Louise knew.

She hadn't got to where she had in Humble Associates by signing whatever piece of paper happened beneath her nose. As was her wont, the first thing she'd done, upon receiving the contract from Celestial Stays, was to carbon copy it over to her lawyer.

Later, she had spoken on the phone with the lawyer, who had highlighted the pertinent parts of the contract, and advised her accordingly.

One of the sections which her lawyer had flagged up was this so-called Customer Care Policy. In fact, Louise had read through the section twice just to be clear on all the points.

When she'd come to finally give her assent to the terms and

conditions, she had been satisfied that she would have no trouble acting in accordance.

But, that said, she had never envisioned a situation like this.

She had never believed that someone would do this to her.

That someone would betray her so horribly.

Again.

"Louise? *Louise?*" Mackenzie jabbered out.

When Louise returned to the present, she saw that Mackenzie was just removing her finger from her inner-ear, having sent out some message or other.

"You are contractually bound to come with me."

Louise held herself still. There was only one way out of this, of course. She would need to resign on the spot . . . but then what would happen?

Back to Earth.

Back to her old life.

Back to her old *haunts*.

Nothing would have changed . . .

As this revelation seeped through Louise's brain, she couldn't help but think of Njhay.

And those gorgeous bronze-green eyes.

That chiselled body.

She would give up whatever future there might be there.

. . . Now where was her mind going?

Louise glanced up at Mackenzie.

Met her eye.

"Okay," she said. "I'll go with you."

Mackenzie smiled. "Good," she replied, and then indicated the corridor outside. "This way please."

As Louise ventured out of the now brilliantly clean lab, she noticed Njhay's glasses, still lying on one of the metal examination tables. Despite the situation, despite what she was about to put herself through, she managed to raise a smile.

She had cleaned around the glasses, left them just as they were . . . with the smudge marks and all.

That way Njhay could be sure it hadn't been a droid that'd cleaned up in here.

11

STERILISATION

*N*jhay *brought his hand up* to his mouth and exhaled onto his palm. He gave it a sniff. He really needed to go freshen up, at least to gargle some mouthwash. But he was afraid that he didn't have time. He had so much to get through in preparation for Zito's visit.

And he already felt so far behind.

He trotted along the corridor, coming up to his lab.

He was only a couple of steps from the door when he recalled how Louise had turned up in the lab just before he'd left. His heart throbbed. His stomach dipped. Now he really *could* do with locating some mouthwash—from *somewhere* . . .

He glanced about desperately, but, of course, not so much as a single bottle presented itself.

His earpiece gave him a nudge.

Reminded him that he had places to be.

Things to *arrange*.

'Love', he supposed, would have to wait—if it was really on the cards at all.

Taking a deep breath, he stepped through the doorway, and into the lab. He glanced about, rendered stunned for several moments. It was spotless. The whole *place* was spotless.

He crunched his eyes shut, then opened them again, hoping to have cleared the illusion which had surely been plaguing his vision.

He turned his attention down to the table, seeing his glasses there.

He'd been looking all over for them.

He snatched them up, puffing over each lens in turn and then giving them a rigorous rub with his overalls. He set the glasses over the bridge of his nose, and the world came to him sharply once again.

The first thing he noted was how the lab was cleaner than he'd thought to begin with. And, second, he realised there was absolutely no sign of Louise anywhere.

She had gone.

Only when his heart sank did he realise how truly disappointed he was.

His earpiece nudged him again, prodding him about the precariously balanced schedule he had set himself in anticipation of Zito's visit.

With a slight weight in his gut, he glanced about the lab, feeling as if he was leaving his home behind. Then he ventured out, turning the lights off as he went.

GIRL TALK

*W*hen *Mackenzie* led her off to meet with a PEAR, Louise was surprised to find that it wasn't empty; that there was another passenger awaiting them:

Wendy.

Suddenly unsure, Louise held back from the PEAR's opening visor.

She found herself on the fierce end of a prod in the lower back, courtesy of Mackenzie.

"Get in," Mackenzie said, in a not-particularly-reassuring way.

But Louise did as she was told.

She perched on the seat of the PEAR, scooting herself up against Wendy's outer thigh.

"Heidi ho!" Wendy said, laying on the levity.

"Hi," Louise replied.

Mackenzie got in on the other side of the PEAR, and the visor came down upon them.

Louise realised she was trapped.

Between the two women.

The PEAR took off, barrelling through the air.

Feeling the silence thickening around her, Louise couldn't help but give in to the urge to break it. "Where're we going?"

"Nowhere in particular," Mackenzie replied, rapid-fire.

Although Louise had her answer, she couldn't say that she found it reassuring. She decided that a follow-up question was required. "Are we going to the landing strip—to meet Costantino Zito?"

"Eventually," Mackenzie said.

Then Wendy chimed in, "But first we've got to talk."

Louise's stomach tightened. " 'Talk' ? . . . About what?"

Wendy and Mackenzie exchanged a knowing glance.

Louise couldn't help but feel that she'd got herself caught in the middle of a well-executed pincer movement.

Mackenzie stuck her finger into her ear, and even Louise could tell what order she was issuing, because the PEAR—acting on Mackenzie's instructions—banked sharply to the right and settled down on a bare patch of lunar dust . . . the middle of nowhere as far as the Dome was concerned.

In the distance, Louise could make out the Lunar Grand, the Stellar Tide Casino alongside it.

Slowly, gradually, the *hum* of the PEAR's engines gave way.

And there was silence.

Wendy and Mackenzie turned their attention inward.

Their full focus on Louise.

"All right," Mackenzie said. "Time for you to spill the goods."

Wide-eyed, doing her best to appear innocent of any contrivance, Louise replied, "What 'goods' ?"

This was simply met with a pair of chiding glares, one from each side.

This time Wendy took up the slack in the conversation. "We want to know your history—we want to know why you're trying to keep your relationship with Humble Associates a secret."

Again, Louise felt her whole body seize tight.

"What is it?" Mackenzie said, for the first time seeming to be solely interested in Louise, and not with half of her mind on something happening at the other end of the Dome . . . ready to jab her finger into her ear to issue an order to someone—or *something*.

When Louise didn't reply right away, Wendy broke in.

"It's a man, isn't it?"

Louise held herself very still.

And then blinked.

She felt a hand on her left thigh.

When she looked, she realised it was Mackenzie.

The touch was out of step when considering Mackenzie's usual subtlety—about as subtle as a rubber hammer applied to the forehead. The touch was reassuring, tender—*understanding*.

Both women, Louise realised, were regarding her with wide eyes.

If their intention was to feign pleasantry so that they might extract Louise's Deepest, Darkest Secrets, then they were doing a fairly good job of it.

"Who was he?" Mackenzie said. "What did he *do*?"

For the first time, Louise felt as if there was a shred of sympathy in Mackenzie's voice.

Louise still felt as if she was blocked—as if there was something *physically blocking* her throat. She waited for it to clear. But it remained where it was.

"Another woman?" Wendy put in. "I can give counsel on that, if you'll be kind enough to excuse any choice language which might sneak out."

"Let's give her space," Mackenzie said, and although the sentiment was a kind one, it wasn't all that practical given that the interior of this PEAR wasn't exactly spacious for a sole occupant.

With a trio it was positively crowded.

Louise felt her heart beating hard against her ribs. Blood rushed to her temples. It felt as if her whole body was fighting to escape; to simply bust through the visor and run out across the lunar plains, back for the Basements where she would lock herself in her room:

Like some teenage girl.

Well, if she *was* going to open up about her past, she couldn't see herself having a better opportunity than right now. She drew in a shaky breath, stared out across the plains.

"I'd just got through with university," she began. "I was twenty-two years old . . . and I was looking for a job." Already feeling a little light-headed, she drew in a profound breath. "Like the rest, I headed to London to find a job. I rented a room in this draughty old Victorian house, hardly within range of the Link, and I set about looking."

Louise felt the grip on her thigh squeeze a touch tighter.

She glanced around and was greeted by a smile from Mackenzie.

It filled her with good feeling.

She allowed herself to ease into the story a little further, to reopen all of those wounds which hadn't had so much as a chance to heal.

"I met him on a rainy Tuesday in a café. He was . . ." here she paused for several moments, finding the right word ". . . *charming*."

She couldn't help but smile.

Even after all that had happened, she just *couldn't* help it.

"He asked to buy me a coffee, and, well, you know how it goes, we got talking, and I told him about how I was searching for a job —told him about my past experience, I . . . I don't *know* . . ."

She trailed off and received a squeeze of her thigh—from Mackenzie—and, as a bonus, a squeeze of her shoulder—from Wendy. She breathed out a sigh.

"I was still wet behind the ears in so many ways . . . and I guess, until this past year, until everything came crumbling down, I still was . . ." She tried out a smile. It felt okay. "It's really taken me time," she went on, "time to come to terms with just what happened."

"What *did* happen?" Mackenzie put in, not out of impatience to get this over with, but more out of eagerness to help.

To help Louise.

Louise continued, "Well, of course he revealed who he was, this grand executive at Humble Associates. He offered me a good place at the company. And I worked hard, and, well . . ."

"He put the clampers on you," Wendy said, butting in.

Louise noted the scowl which went sizzling across from Mackenzie.

Despite being fully two decades her elder, Wendy buttoned her lip.

Louise went on, "I thought that my progress through Humble Associates was because of my hard work—I was naïve enough to think that . . . to think that I was just like anybody else, that it was something *inconsequential* that I was carrying on this 'thing' with this *man* . . . but, I don't know."

She shook her head.

"It all seemed so obvious to me at the time, and, in the same way, it all seems so obvious to me right now; just what he was pulling on me. With each successive promotion, I thought it was down to my own efforts, I thought that I was 'getting on' in the company, I'd been there for a full six years, after all . . . but, then . . ."

"A younger model appeared?" Wendy said, apparently unable to help herself, despite Mackenzie's reprimand.

"Well," Louise said, allowing the reply to linger, "*not so much* . . . you could say, I suppose, that *various* younger models had already appeared, or that they'd been on the scene the whole time. But it wasn't just that—"

A lump formed in her throat; but she knew she couldn't put what she was thinking into words; not yet . . . not until she knew Mackenzie and Wendy a little better.

"It wasn't *just* that," Louise repeated, hoping Mackenzie and Wendy might not notice.

Here, and Louise couldn't prevent it from happening; she felt herself beginning to tear up . . . but she swallowed the tears down, knowing that she had already cried far too many tears for *him*.

Both Mackenzie and Wendy seemed able to read her mind . . . more squeezes.

Louise was capable of keeping the tears away, but the anger was a different matter altogether. Acting instinctively, she slapped herself on the forehead. She watched the red dots scatter across her vision. "*Idiot!*" she said.

Neither Mackenzie or Wendy said anything at all.

"He strung me along," Louise continued, after a brief pause. "The last time we were together he said he saw me as 'wife material' . . . thankfully someone in the office was merciful, they saw fit to tell me what was really going on; to lay it all out for me with irrefutable evidence."

Again, she shook her head, both unable to believe what had occurred, and that she was relating it right now.

"I never saw him again after I found out . . . and I've been running away ever since." She glanced up, met both Wendy and Mackenzie's watchful eyes. "One day, though, I couldn't help but comb through the Link, to check out what he was up to." She shook her head. "Apparently at Humble Associates they don't care all that much about personal considerations because they made him the managing director." She paused, collected herself together. "But the worst part is that he's doing it all over again; another impressionable young girl; stringing her along—promising her love—delivering only deception . . ."

There was a long silence.

When Louise finally thought to glance at Mackenzie, she was surprised to see her smiling from ear to ear. " 'Delivering only deception' ?" Mackenzie said. "I'll have to remember that one; nice line, sums up so many people so appropriately."

Louise glanced over at Wendy, and was surprised to see that she was more pensive than Mackenzie; that she was far more introspective. Although Louise really knew very little about either woman's life, she had already drawn the conclusion that while Mackenzie was no doubt more wild to the wind—happy to pick 'em up, then kick 'em to the curb—Wendy had had a lot more invested in her husband than she had let on with the matter-of-fact recounting of her past history.

Finally, Wendy spoke up. "Say his name," she said, and then met Louise's eye. "Don't make him into some god or *devil* . . . you put him on a pedestal by not saying his name."

Although Louise felt a strange satisfaction at having vented so thoroughly to these two women, she couldn't help but feel a fresh tension rack her body. She wanted to draw a line under this whole ordeal . . . never talk about it again, if at all possible.

She was surprised to look at Mackenzie and see that she was just as eager as Wendy for Louise to speak her ex-lover's name. And, because it seemed like such a silly thing . . . such a *silly* request . . . she decided to do so. What could it hurt?

"Alex," Louise said, remarking at her cool, collected tone. "Alex *Barn*."

13

LAUNCH QUEUE

*D*ressed in the dirty-grey coloured flight suit, Alex Barn tilted his neck back and took in the serpentine queue leading into the space elevator. He was right at the back.

He *and* his beautiful fiancée, Fiona.

Usually, whenever Alex's celebrity couldn't quite cut it—when he wasn't instantly recognised whilst making an impulsive visit to a restaurant or bar—he could depend on Fiona's stunning figure, her flowing auburn hair, her flawless sense of style, and, above all, her ability to flutter those voluptuous eyelashes of hers. That would, without exception, get them through the door in swift fashion.

Now, though, this didn't seem an option.

The Launch Centre officials all seemed quite sombre individuals.

As the managing director of Humble Associates, he'd become accustomed to a life of sleek personal transporters waiting for him at every curb; people on hand looking after his every desire; and, it went without saying, doors flying open for him.

A 'queue', however, was an unpleasant fact that had to be faced given the circumstances; since he'd settled on the Moon as being his destination of choice for his first holiday in four years.

He had to be content with the fact that he was no longer a big fish in a small tank.

In fact, it was as if the tank had been tossed unmercifully into the sea and he now found himself surrounded on all sides by sharks.

Yes, it was an unpleasant truth, but a truth all the same. For the first time this decade, Alex Barn felt somewhat intimidated by the company he was keeping.

It had been a long flight from London to reach Aranuka; an atoll of the island nation of Kiribati, in the Pacific Ocean, where the Launch Centre was located.

Although the hospitality on arrival had been warm, it certainly hadn't been anywhere approaching the one-hundred-per-cent bespoke level he'd grown to expect.

He had noted, on several occasions, how he'd been asked for his name, and—on one *unforgettable* occasion—asked to repeat it.

However, some sort of business-like deference had stopped him from becoming angry at this slight. He had to admit that he himself had been rendered somewhat star struck by the sixteen-person strong roster of which he formed a part.

Why, there'd been Anders Morlachek, of Silvertonnes Industries; an Ex-European Federation Presidential Nominee. And then there'd been Gunta Dani, the founder and manager of Evocative Flavours; famous for its milk-chocolate recipe, attempts at which to reverse engineer had been made for over a century now, and without luck.

Alex even had an EvoBar, their best-selling product, in his hand luggage for the trip.

He certainly couldn't get enough of them.

And *zero* calories too!

Finally, and this probably did cap off the whole list, there was Costantino Zito; the mogul who could boast a device bearing his name in just about every single home across the entirety of the face of the Earth, and—Alex was certain—the *Moon* too.

Yes, Alex had to admit that he was in illustrious company, and, in a strange way, he was glad to stand aside and watch better beings than himself reap the benefits of their success.

So much could not, however, be said for his fiancée.

Arms folded across her chest, Fiona's pout resembled a minor land fault. She flexed up onto the tips of her toes to get a better look at the unmoving line of people ahead. Then she sighed at Alex, as if *he* was supposed to do something about it.

Alex only put on a bemused expression, shrugged. "Sorry," he said. "Nothing to be done."

Fiona gave another sigh, and then reached up for her hair, which she'd been forced to tuck into a bun to accommodate the helmet. There were few things which Fiona liked less than having to 'tame' her hair, as Alex well knew. It made her irritable.

Alex slipped the queue a sidelong glance, not wanting to meet anybody's eye in particular, worried that it might bring him into that most embarrassing of executive-level business situations:

Having to explain just *who* he was . . .

He watched on as one of the Launch Officials checked Gunta Dani's flight suit, looking over whatever needed to be looked over. Apparently content—*mercy of all mercies*—the Launch Official waved her through, on into the space elevator.

The queue shuffled forward.

Alex risked a glance to Fiona, and caught a frown for his trouble.

He only smiled.

He knew that, once on the Moon—once Fiona realised just *what* a romantic gesture this was—she would lighten up; she would melt in his arms all over again . . . just as she had done when he'd lined her up with that role of Public Relations Manager at Humble Associates.

He had long ago determined that she was *most definitely* wife material.

It seemed an almost inconsequential step that soon enough she would see that *he* was her future.

"Mister Barn? Alex Barn?"

Alex felt a tingle pass up his spine. It seemed as if—just for a couple of seconds—before he could regain his composure, every single muscle in his body seized up. Alex found himself whipped back to his school days, to back when he'd been a timid schoolboy, struck dumb whenever the teacher called on him to speak out loud in class . . . he had banished that school boy to the graveyard of the past so long ago. Or so it had seemed.

When he turned, he found himself eye-to-eye with none other than Costantino Zito—he of the Zito multimedia empire; of the Zito Entertainment Unit. Alex busied himself taking in every last detail of the man's appearance:

The cool, shoulder-height, bluish-grey hair.

The firm, raised cheekbones.

The well-adventured, tanned skin.

Above all else, that winning ear-to-ear smile.

"It is Alex Barn, is it not?" Zito said, his head cocked to one side.

Alex continued to feel somewhat sideswiped by this turn of events.

Finally, he noted the outstretched hand.

He eyed it, and then reached down to shake.

He even managed to summon—from *somewhere*—his practised businessman's smile.

"Yes," Alex finally replied, "that's right."

Zito broke off the firm, efficient shake. He formed a double-barrelled gun with his fingers and pointed it at Alex's chest. "Humble," he said, neatly, concisely.

Alex almost forgot himself.

Thankfully, he recovered just in time.

"Humble Associates, yes," he said.

"I love your work in Humble Kitchens," Zito said. "At home, at my family home in Argentina, we have one of the, uh . . ."

There was a brief pause while Zito apparently searched for the appropriate word. When he found it, he snapped his fingers, making Alex flinch.

"*Menthol Grills*," Zito said.

It was a kneejerk reaction masquerading as confidence, but Alex spewed out the sales pitch all the same. "The Menthol Grill was developed according to the most stringent of market research. It was our intention not only to produce a product which would become a kitchen staple, but one which, quite simply, would be synonymous with the Great Summer Barbecue."

Already—even though Alex wouldn't have been able to help himself if he'd tried—he winced at this regurgitation. He was certain that Costantino Zito got far more than his fair share of marketing talk all day at the office; and he hardly wanted it now . . . while he was setting off on holiday.

However, to Alex's surprise, Zito's whole face creased up in a wild smile. He slipped a brief glance at Fiona, then looked back at Alex. "Fascinating," he said. "My mother *loves* the Menthol Grill, and, as I am sure you can tell"—he patted a non-existent paunch at his stomach—"I am quite the fan also." He again made a gun of his fingers, this time pointing it at Alex's temple. "Really, I do like the way your mind works and I would be very interested in taking these conversations further. There are certain, ah . . . *opportunities* that you and Humble might welcome." Here he whipped his hand up in the air, as if to pull thoughts from the ether. "I believe that there are some quite well-organised plans being put in place for mine and my son's visit."

Here Alex noted the *man* standing a few paces away, dressed in his flight suit; a carbon copy of Costantino Zito from twenty years earlier.

The famous *Gofreddo* Zito.

What teenage boy hadn't fantasised what it might be like to stand in *his* shoes?

Alex turned back into Zito, who had something else to say.

"My PA was in touch with somebody from Humble, somebody up on the Moon. They have offered to help show me around." He smiled again. "A very nice *personal* touch, I must say."

Here Alex had to admit that he was at a loss. He couldn't think of anybody at all involved with Humble up on Luna, but, then again, Humble *was* a big company. It could just as easily have been someone trying to impress; someone who'd maybe worked a week in the Post Room and decided to embellish their curriculum vitae.

"Mister Barn . . ."

"Alex, please."

"*Alex*," Zito said, his whole mouth flexing around Alex's name, as if he was testing how it sounded to his ear. "It seems almost as if it is fated—as if Humble and Zito should be walking hand-in-hand on the lunar surface." He paused a moment then added, "Would you be interested in accompanying me throughout the visit?"

Although he knew it to be the biggest cliché of all, Alex believed he was dreaming. It didn't surprise him completely when Fiona gave him a light pinch on the underside of his arm. From the sting of it, Alex could state—categorically—that this was *indeed* all happening. And if this little foray hadn't been enough for Alex to die happy, then the fact that the queue broke out of its lethargy and began to make trudging progress forward was as good as a personal assurance that he'd made it to heaven.

"That, Señor Zito, sounds a wonderful prospect."

Zito screwed up his features as if he'd had the misfortune to taste something deeply objectionable. He held up a palm. "Please," he said, "call me *Tino.*"

Alex was fairly certain that he had gone *beyond* heaven by that point . . .

14

ON PARADE

As Louise stood straight-backed and smartly dressed in her royal-blue, Celestial Stays overalls, she couldn't help but feel as if she'd been recruited as some sort of a space cadet. She recalled, back when she'd been a teenager, how she'd had fantasies about running away from home, doing something as ridiculous as this . . . putting her name forward to venture off into unknown frontiers.

That sense of adventure clung to her still.

That sense of adventure had surely nudged her into making the decision to come to the Moon.

And a larger sense of adventure kept her here now.

From the top of her scalp, all the way down to her toenails, she could feel herself lightly trembling. In a matter of minutes, she would be working as a personal bridge between Celestial Stays and Costantino Zito. And she'd hardly been up on the Moon for a week.

As she'd been carefully instructed by Mackenzie, Louise kept her eyes fixed on a point in mid-air. She wasn't to allow her mind to drift. She was to keep herself ready to be called upon at any moment. She knew the Airlock doors would slide open any time now; that Costantino Zito would arrive to pass through Entry Clearance.

Keeping her mind unoccupied was much more difficult than she had imagined. Her eyes kept on drifting to those who stood opposite her, the many Guardians—all of them with the same silver badge Louise had hurriedly been presented by Mackenzie.

Mackenzie had reasoned the matter away by saying that it would look 'odd' if Louise hadn't made it to being a Guardian, but Louise knew that it meant more, too.

It meant that, although Mackenzie might still see her as a threat, it didn't mean she was going to treat her unfairly. There was a spirit of competition, but, also, there was a strong sense of fairness.

The fact that Louise couldn't care *less* about 'getting on' within the Celestial Stays structure seemed beside the point at this juncture.

As she took in the Guardians standing opposite, she noted some of the names.

Of course, Wendy Flowme and Alicia Brennan were among them, but it was the others who Louise took a second look at now. The ones who Mackenzie had hurriedly introduced her to.

There was Julius Denisov; a Russian who worked high up in the Stellar Tide Casino. There was something about his sneer-eyed expression which Louise didn't much care for. And he was wearing a rose pinned just above his Guardian's badge like some kind of space dandy. Beyond that, though, she could see no reason for disliking him.

She hadn't so much as spoken to him.

Then there was Miguel Cruz; a Mexican with buzz-cut hair and stubble. The collar of his overalls had been pulled up to cover the tattoos which crawled down the back of his neck.

She couldn't help wondering to herself if the tattoo stretched the entirety of his body.

He seemed an unlikely sort to be running the Armstrong Archive, but, as Mackenzie had assured her, after they'd been introduced, he was *very much* overqualified for the role.

Finally, of those who Louise could recall, there was Parick Fourie, from South Africa.

A pilot who proudly ran a Lunar Shuttle at breakneck speeds across the plains for the more thrill-seeking of the guests.

At least Louise could say one thing about these men, and it was that they were all roughly the same age as she was—all of them in about their late-twenties to early-thirties. To the unknowing eye, she surely didn't look out of place as a Guardian.

As she turned her attention back to the Airlock doors, she couldn't help but think about Njhay, and how he had never made it to being a Guardian . . . and all because—in his own words—he refused to play the 'game'.

She couldn't help speculating how accurate of a statement that was.

Could there be some *other* reason?

Those familiar half dozen chimes sounded in her inner-ear, and that was all she knew before the Airlock doors slid back; to reveal the most distinguished of guests.

At first, Louise couldn't keep her thoughts straight. Although she'd been expressly instructed to keep her gaze neutral—to not *stare* at the celebrity guests—she couldn't help but gawp . . . just a little. This *was* Costantino Zito, after all . . .

Louise hadn't been briefed on the others, on Anders Morlachek, former European Federation Presidential Nominee; or, for that matter, Gunta Dani, of those fabulously addictive EvoBars . . . one of Louise's few vices down on Earth; thankfully, for whatever explanation there was, EvoBars hadn't yet made their way up onto the Moon.

She watched on as the Guardians assigned to these two behemoths swept them off, taking them under their wings for the duration of Entry Clearance. And then, before Louise had really got herself under control—and still shaking without any apparent end —she found herself standing almost nose-to-nose with the man himself.

Costantino Zito.

Time seemed to move slower. It seemed that she had impossibly long moments to absorb every aspect of his face. To take in that flowing, blue-grey hair of his. The warmly tanned skin. And those laugh lines collected around his eyes; engrained in his handsome, muscular cheeks. "And you must be *Louise*," Zito got out.

Louise remembered herself.

She snatched a breath.

Smiled.

"Yes," she said, "that's correct, Señor Zito."

Costantino Zito held up his hand. " 'Tino'," he corrected her, gently, before turning and revealing, behind his shoulder, a man almost in his exact image; aged in his late-twenties rather than his late-fifties. "My son, Gofreddo."

Gofreddo Zito, apparently not missing a beat, took a stride forward. He clenched hold of Louise's hand in a firm, unmoving grip. His eyes didn't leave hers as he shook. "Call me 'Fred', please. It is wonderful to make your acquaintance."

Of course Louise had heard *all about* Gofreddo Zito . . . some form of his image seemed to garner just about every gossip outlet on at least a bi-weekly basis.

Gofreddo captured bursting from some nightclub, a girl on each arm.

Or else photographed among presidential spawn—'the Great and the Good'—attending this or that black-tie dinner; everyone around him in stitches of laughter.

Gofreddo was *always* centre stage.

And he was the suitor of his father's empire.

However, Louise found herself only ensnared by Gofreddo's charms for a matter of seconds, because her gaze inevitably moved beyond him.

To the man and woman standing right on his shoulder.

Of course, she recognised them both straightaway.

Alex Barn.

And his new woman:

Fiona Adams.

Neither of them saw Louise. She hoped to duck away from them—to somehow whisk 'Fred' and 'Tino' off to Entry Clearance.

But, as she attempted just that, Costantino Zito held up his finger. "Hang on," he said, "I do believe that you should know one another."

He cracked out a glistening smile; one which, at any other time, Louise was certain she would've found to be striding the line between alluring and captivating.

Now, though, it only brought on nausea.

Before Louise could squirm free of the inevitable collision,

Costantino Zito stood back and waited for Alex Barn to close on her.

Alex . . . *her* Alex . . . the one who had *been* her Alex.

"Yes," Alex said, through a thin-lipped smile. "I *do* believe I recognise you."

Alex's hand was cool, slightly damp.

He kept his wrist limp.

No strength to it.

"Lauren, uh, Lorna . . . ?"

"*Louise,*" she corrected him, like he needed it.

Alex smiled wider. His hand slithered free of hers.

When Louise turned her attention upward—to Fiona standing on Alex's shoulder—she saw that the current Public Relations Manager of Humble Associates had no intention of putting on an act.

Her loathing of Louise was there for anybody to see.

As if sensing this, Costantino Zito clapped his hands together with a neat *slap.* He smiled wider still, as if smiling was all it would take to fill in the deep fissures here. "I think we should get to the hotel," he said. "Give everyone a chance to freshen up, hmm?"

15

BREAKDOWN

Louise brought the toilet cubicle door shut with a firm *slam*. She brought the toilet seat down and sat upon it. The ebbing, burbling electronic music piped through the Lunar Grand at this time of day, lightly caressing her temples. Her brain felt beyond fried. Her heart felt almost as if it might bounce free of her ribcage. She wasn't entirely certain that she would be able to find her feet again.

Her mind spiralled with what had just unfolded; how she had guided Costantino Zito, and his son, up to their respective suites before being forced into showing Alex and Fiona to their own.

Once they had been alone, not one of them had spoken, of course.

What would there have been to say? . . . It wasn't like Alex had been in any position to ask just what had happened when Louise had decided to run off . . . and Louise *really* didn't want to know anything about the arrangement which Fiona shared with Alex.

The same one *she* had shared with Alex.

Outside, Louise heard the firm *slap* of rubber soles against tile. She stared at the small gap at the bottom of the toilet cubicle and saw the legs, wrapped in the royal-blue overalls. She could almost anticipate the pair of knocks on the door.

"Louise?"

It was Wendy.

"Can I come in?"

Louise held herself very still, as if Wendy might somehow come to believe that Louise wasn't in there at all. If only disappearing was so easy.

In the end, she knew it was inevitable she would have to open up, so she did so.

Wendy stepped inside the cubicle, locking it behind her.

She wore a sympathetic expression. But Louise really didn't *want* sympathy. She only wanted to be left alone with her thoughts. To think through just what a mess she'd made of her life, and, worse, how she had run away from her problems, like some little girl; not a woman at all . . . certainly not worthy of anybody's love or respect.

Wendy leaned casually up against the closed cubicle door. She inspected her nails as if this was a normal place to conduct a fair-minded chat. "That's him?" she said. "Alex *Barn*?"

When Louise had first got here, into the cubicle, she thought she might cry. But there was nothing left. She had already cried so much . . .

"Well," Wendy went on, "if you'll forgive me for saying, he looks like a real yuppie scumbag."

Despite the gravity of the situation, Louise couldn't help but smirk at this remark.

And then *chuckle*.

"And that piece he's got on his arm, well, she looks like she knows a career opportunity when she sees one."

"That makes two of us," Louise couldn't help putting in, her voice not quite as shaky as she'd first thought it might be.

Wendy drew a deep breath. "You think you're going to be okay? I mean, it'll be a week of this . . . a week with *them*."

That was just about the last thing Louise wanted to hear. It felt as if the ground beneath her feet opened wide. Her brain couldn't help but stick at the prospect of sharing so much as another moment with Alex Barn and the soon-to-be Mrs Barn.

"Listen," Wendy said, "there's two ways you can go out of this that I can figure."

Louise glanced up, catching Wendy's unshakable stare . . . *God*, what Louise wouldn't give to have Wendy's matter-of-fact resilience right now . . . what she wouldn't have given to have Wendy's well-earned distance from the world; a way in which she could no longer feel pain.

"Go on," Louise replied.

"Shuttle's returning tomorrow morning—first thing." Wendy gave a shrug. "If you like, I can get you a seat on it. After what you told me and Mackenzie, I'm sure we could shake it."

Louise felt something within her leap at Wendy.

Something deep and unmovable telling her—*yelling for her*—to get away . . . to *escape*.

And, yeah, that'd worked *so well* so far, hadn't it?

"The other way?" Louise said.

Wendy smirked. "You can suck it up. This stays between you and me. You put on your *pro* face, grin and bear it . . . do whatever you can to honour that contract you signed; the one which commits you to providing—*to the best of your ability*—an outstand-ing, once-in-a-lifetime experience at the Celestial Stays Dome."

Louise thought Wendy had finished there, but she kept going.

"And when you wave them all back into their Shuttle, you'll know that you won—you'll have *beaten* whatever it is that's been eating at you for all this time. You'll be the envy of so many of us because you'll have that ever elusive thing." Wendy's smile drooped slightly. "*Closure.*"

Closure . . . was that the answer?

Why she'd run so far?

And what good had it done?

Wendy straightened up. She rolled her shoulders, apparently loosening some tension which'd worked itself in there. Then she reached out and unlocked the toilet cubicle door.

Opened it wide.

"There it is," Wendy said. "You can go whichever way you want."

Louise stared out through the doorway.

Sank her teeth into her lower lip.

And couldn't help wondering whether she could do this.

Whether she could *really* do this.

"Mind made up?" Wendy added.

Louise met her eye, then smiled.

She nodded.

"Good," Wendy said, and then dug into her overall pockets, "because I've got some emergency supplies." She paused. "Now, don't get me wrong, you *will* still be wearing those Celestial Stays overalls, but, at the very least, we can twist that hair of yours into something a little more fierce."

It seemed out of place at first. But it soon proved irresistible.

A warm glow had taken hold of her.

And it was getting hotter all the time.

16

CELEBRATION PREPARATIONS

Even though Njhay knew that everything was in place—
that he'd taken care of all of the moving pieces of the
puzzle—that there was *absolutely nothing* which could go wrong, he
couldn't quite manage to convince his writhing hands.

He stood by as the Guardians escorted the distinguished guests
along the path of the Crescent Gardens. All the guests wore the
burgundy visitors' overalls, with a platinum badge—as if it was
required—confirming the fact that they were, indeed, 'VISITORS'.

As the Dome lights gradually dimmed in their imitation of the
twenty-four-hour Earth clock, Njhay could tell that the guests
were looking somewhat tired following the day's activities. He
supposed that they'd been taken on the full tour.

Although he tried his very best to stay out of the Hospitality
side of things, he knew the basic routine.

For most of the morning, the guests would've been allowed to
relax in their hotel suites; coming round from the journey.

Later, they would have been treated to the Armstrong Archive, while their attention spans allowed them to take in some history.

Next, for a change of pace, they'd have been swept off across the lunar plains for a breakneck trip in a Shuttle, stopping by for a sombre visit to the Lunar One crash site . . . the greatest tragedy the Moon had known . . .

They had come to the Crescent Gardens at 'twilight', for some unspecified entertainment.

And, if Njhay knew anything at all about Hospitality, he knew that the guests would be taken off to the Stellar Tide Casino for the evening where they could blow all those many, many credits that rich people seemed so keen to throw away.

Yes, he was quite convinced that he'd become jaded at the prospect of a prolonged stay on the Moon. He'd had a good time up here—got some interesting *work* done—but it was undoubtedly past time that he move onto the next thing.

Why, he felt almost as if he'd forgotten about *everything* that'd happened down on Earth.

Almost . . .

He only traced the surface of the faces passing by. He couldn't help but admire his own ability to not see—to *not care about*—the faces. It had taken him a long while to become this detached from the real world. He would never—*ever*—go back to being connected again.

With that thought on his mind—and with another part of his brain readying to send the order through his neural transmitter which would spark the whole show into life—he couldn't help but recognise one of the faces within the crowd.

Costantino Zito.

No matter how hard Njhay tried to distance himself from that most human of qualities—*pattern recognition*—he realised that it was in vain.

He would *always* be human after all . . .

Just as he supposed every other Earthling's brain was, his was engrained with the image of Costantino Zito's face. Of that steady curve of well-blooded lips; of sweeping, never-thinning hair.

How he seemed to have a smile for *everybody*.

If he had ever been asked to personify success in pictorial form, he knew that whatever sketch he drew would come out as something along the lines of Costantino Zito.

As Costantino Zito—apparently sensing somebody was watching him—turned in his direction, Njhay looked away.

And who should his gaze fall upon?

Louise.

At first, he couldn't quite believe what he was seeing. It had taken him a couple of heartbeats just to confirm to himself that she was who he *thought* she was . . . the woman who he had hardly stopped thinking about—*dreaming about*—for the past week.

It was something about her appearance . . . something that was *different* about her today.

And then he realised it was her hair.

He absorbed how it was layered and lush, and *not* pulled up in a bun or a ponytail as it had been throughout her days working in the Crescent Gardens.

If he'd been forced to put his finger on an exact description, he might've used the word 'elemental' to better pin the image down.

There was something *elemental* about her.

Slowly, she turned her gaze to him.

And he felt something grip hold of his stomach.

Twist it around.

So long . . . it'd been so long since he'd felt like this . . .

For a long time her blue eyes held him.

He felt his breathing shallow, and then stop completely.

It was only when she widened her eyes—when she snapped back to something which Costantino Zito was saying—that Njhay remembered himself.

He blinked away his daze then set his mind to the task at hand.

He activated the display.

17

ACTIVATION

*T*hough *Louise* would hardly have claimed it to be a pleasant situation, even she had to admit that it hadn't been quite as bad as she'd made it out.

Sure, she was balancing her ex-boyfriend and former colleague with one of the foremost celebrities the world had ever known; and of course she was contractually bound for the two of them to have a 'good time' while up here, beneath the Celestial Stays Dome . . . but, it seemed, as the Hospitality Division had laid out the plans for the day, that just about everything had gone swimmingly.

It had been a tour just as much for Louise as it had been for the guests.

Once they'd got the guests outfitted for their visitors' overalls— a burgundy colour with no-nonsense, platinum 'VISITORS' badges stitched to their breast pockets—they had visited the Armstrong Archive. They had been placed in the capable hands of Miguel Cruz who had taken them through various exhibits showing off the length and breadth of lunar history.

Next, they had been whisked away on Patrick Fourie's Shuttle, who had brought out white knuckles even from the world-weary, hardy adventurer, Gofreddo Zito.

When Louise had somehow found it within herself to make a quip about 'Fred's' reputation for all kinds of recklessness and debauchery, he had only responded with a smile and a none-too-convincing reply that he had only been 'mildly concerned'.

Throughout the day, Louise had been worried about the moment when Costantino Zito would bring up her history with Humble Associates, believing that all her secrets would be revealed; but, thus far, he hadn't made so much as a murmur about Humble.

Alex and Fiona had, for the most part, stayed toward the back of their select group.

Only getting involved when prompted to by Costantino.

The day had got them as far as here, the Crescent Gardens, where Louise had explained how she herself had been working on the Gardens—keeping things in order—though she'd taken great pains to insist that she had nothing to do personally with what was about to unfold.

In fact, she really hadn't *any* idea about what Njhay had in store.

Just to think about him made her heart clench like a fist.

It gave her a kick of adrenalin.

She glanced back off to where she had seen him, looking slightly worried in that away-with-the-fairies manner of his. He wasn't there any longer.

She felt a swelling emptiness within her chest.

Something within her pined to be with him.

To be *close* to him.

To have his *strong arms* wrapped around her.

And then, just when Louise felt as if she was going to begin to shake, or that she would need to desert her guests to go and locate Njhay . . . to *rip* the clothes off the unsuspecting boy's back . . . the light within the Celestial Stays Dome dimmed all the way down.

To night.

She had time to catch her breath as the world began to glow around her.

As the *plants*—in unison—started to glow.

Before she knew what was happening, a milky-white glow illuminated the world as completely as midday. When she caught sight of Costantino Zito's face in profile—as she had done often throughout the day—she saw he was smiling widely; those bright eyes of his twinkling out from within their sockets.

She couldn't help thinking of how she often viewed obscenely successful businessmen such as Costantino. She had always thought of them as being no-nonsense, po-faced individuals with only one aim in mind:

To make money.

. . . And yet, Costantino seemed to take genuine pleasure in human warmth; in human *accomplishment*. He seemed to find the good in everybody and everything.

She recalled seeing the tears in his eyes as they'd visited the Lunar One Monument. And not crocodile tears conjured for a camera . . . there were no cameras . . .

She couldn't help but wonder if he'd been so perceptive as to note the tension between herself and Alex, and to say nothing. If that was the truth, then she was glad for his kindness.

She was glad for his *mercy*.

When it seemed the plants could become no brighter—that the milky-white glow couldn't possibly be exceeded—some of them began to fade away. Others flickered.

Louise held her breath.

She traced the illuminated patterns of the leaves; of the entirety of the Gardens.

It was hard to believe that this was the product of long hours of study at a microscope, that Njhay, glasses perched on his head, had peered through the eyepiece and come up with this.

Just to look around her now, she saw the guests all equally as enraptured as Costantino.

It was hard to believe that Njhay hadn't made it to being a Guardian.

The show continued for another few minutes until—with a final fanfare—the whole garden illuminated with one last, unbe- lievably bright light.

Louise wondered if the light would be seen back on Earth.

Soon enough, it was too bright for her to look at directly.

When the light faded down for the final time, with only a scat- tering of plants to provide the illumination for the Gardens—so the guests could find their way along the paths—Costantino turned to Louise, those same tears in his eyes as he'd had earlier at the Memorial. "Who was the responsible for this display?"

Louise felt her whole body pull tight.

Her mind whipped along on overdrive.

Before she managed an answer, Costantino declared, "I should very much like to take him out to dinner—do you think that could be arranged?"

Breaking free of her stupor, she replied. "Yes, I think so."

18

THE STELLAR TIDE

It being the first time Louise had so much as set foot in the Stellar Tide Casino, she was stumped by the layout. She took in the slot machines, the various card tables. The air smelled thickly of floor polish. When she glanced to the bar, she was certain she saw the barman serving somebody a gin and tonic, although it might just as easily have been only water with a slice of lime . . .

Following Costantino's request—or 'Tino' as he kept insisting she call him—Louise had got in touch with Mackenzie, informing her that he wished to meet with Njhay.

A matter-of-fact reply had informed her that the request would be dealt with 'accordingly'.

. . . Even Njhay could be made to bend to the whim of Costantino Zito.

Julius Denisov—the Guardian who Louise had met earlier on that day—stood at the door of the Stellar Tide. His black hair was well-combed and slicked back with gel. He wore a waistcoat over the top of his Celestial Stays overalls.

He was quick and witty with Costantino, as if he might've been chatting with any stranger back on Earth. He led them off to what Denisov referred to as the 'Banquet Hall', which, Louise soon discovered, featured a comically long table—better suited for a group of a hundred or more—coupled with a large viewing platform for peering out into the depths of space.

She wondered how many moneyed gamblers had ended up here in the early hours of the morning, thinking over their losses, thinking on what could've been if only they'd gone with red; if they hadn't gone and staked it all on *black* . . .

Once seated, the whole room: Costantino, Gofreddo, Alex and Fiona, all went silent.

Louise supposed this was a symptom of the day they'd just had, rushing about from this to the other with almost no room to take a breather.

Now, though, they were nearing the end of their first day's stay on the Moon and everybody was ready to eat something; to take some time to relax.

Costantino ordered them a round of drinks. He went for non-alcoholic, fruit-flavoured beverages; showing Louise that he had no interest in having the 'rules' bent or broken for his benefit. If there really was a possibility of a bottle of wine, or a case of beer, he wanted nothing to do with it.

By the time Louise had neared the bottom of her first glass of what tasted—*to her*—like peach mixed with pineapple, she noted somebody come walking in through the door to the Banquet Hall.

It took her approximately a heartbeat to realise just who it was. *Njhay.*

He wore his Celestial Stays overalls. His black hair hung down in corkscrew curls.

Louise couldn't help wondering if Wendy hadn't got to him before he'd been allowed to join Costantino Zito for dinner.

He flipped a quick, burning glance with those bronze-green eyes of his at Louise, and Louise felt as if the seat might melt away beneath her. As he approached the table, Costantino dabbed his lips with his napkin and then—with a beaming grin—welcomed Njhay heartily.

He made a show of having Njhay take a seat beside him at the head of the table, and then immediately bursting into enthusiastic outpourings about the display they had witnessed that evening; and just how 'marvellous' it had all been.

Not knowing quite where to look throughout this exchange, Louise found herself slipping a glance in Gofreddo's direction. She caught a quick eye-roll which betrayed a son weary of his father's manner.

Next, because she didn't have time to catch herself, her attention slipped onto Alex and Fiona, who she observed sitting silently beside one another, each of them lost to their own thoughts.

Soon enough, a battalion of waiters burst into the Banquet Hall, all of them carrying silver trays.

Louise breathed in the steady, warming scent of salmon; a creamy, cheese sauce accompanying it. She couldn't help but flash back to what Wendy had said about shellfish . . . seafood did seem like something of a rash culinary choice on the Moon.

Once the waiters had retreated, it seemed that any misgivings anybody assembled within the Banquet Hall might have about consuming seafood on the Moon dissipated into thin air.

Everybody—even the charismatic Costantino Zito—tucked into their dinner without so much as a smattering of conversation.

The salmon was cooked to perfection, at that most mysterious, and—for Louise, whenever she'd tried to cook it herself—*elusive* point. That point where it would quite simply melt on the tongue as if it was nothing but warmed sorbet.

As they came to the end of their dinner, and with every face around her betraying emotions of *utter contentment*, Louise noted Njhay once more turning into Costantino and slipping him— judging from Costantino's bellowing laughter—an outrageously funny comment or witty observation.

While Costantino—red-faced, chuckling to himself—buried his mouth in his napkin, Louise caught Njhay's eye. His smile, the one he had pressed on for company, slipped slightly. And his intense bronze-green eyes swam through Louise's.

It felt as if—just for a moment or two—time stopped around her.

As if it was just the two of them in the Banquet Hall.

And then—with the *clink* of a fork on a plate—it all returned.

Once more, Njhay was back to speaking with Costantino.

Their dessert was a deliciously naughty chocolate tart which Louise felt immediately guilty about after she'd taken so much as a bite. When she looked around her, she couldn't help noticing that she was easily the first to finish.

Thankfully, nobody thought to comment on this.

And, if Njhay noticed, then he said nothing.

By the time coffee came around, Louise was almost certain that it was a physical impossibility that anything would be able to get through her lips.

But she was proven wrong.

As the dinner came to an end—and with Louise feeling as though she was ready for a good forty winks—the waiters came by to collect everything up.

When Costantino rose from his seat with a yawn, stretching his arms, apparently ready to retire to his suite, everybody else followed.

As Louise herself got up, she could do nothing to prevent the smouldering stare she caught off Alex and Fiona. But she really saw no reason why they should direct their ire at her; she had, after all, merely eaten her dinner in peace and quiet, with minimal conversation.

It had been Njhay who'd dominated Costantino's attentions.

On their way out of the Banquet Hall, Costantino swooped in to Louise to give her a pair of kisses, one on each cheek. That done, and still a little red-faced from the laughter Njhay had inflicted on him, Costantino took his leave; his son, the heir to his fortune, following closely on his heels.

As Louise stood by, half-hypnotised by the craziness of the day —by the whole *craziness* of this situation—she felt somebody bump into her from behind.

Before she could catch her balance, she was falling.

Louise hit the ground with a damp *thump* and immediately felt a scattering of pain at her temple from where she had struck the floor.

Dazed, she looked up.

She caught sight of Fiona standing over her.

Looking down.

Her flimsy, elegant fingers clutched to her mouth in—what was surely—faux shock.

"Oh, Louise," Fiona said. "I *am* terribly sorry—such a *klutz*."

Louise noticed Alex standing beside Fiona.

He looked indifferent, as if it'd been just *anyone* who'd taken a tumble.

When Louise first felt the strong grip at her elbows, gently easing her up to her feet, she believed that it was Gofreddo Zito, that he'd hung back from his father and, hearing her fall, come to help her regain her balance.

But, no; of course it wasn't.

Alex and Fiona wouldn't have been so bold as to try something so base within Costantino's—*or one of his closest aide's*—sight.

It could easily ruin their reputation for ever.

Back on her feet, feeling steady once more, Louise felt the hold on her seize tighter.

When she turned to look, she saw that it was Njhay. He stood there, a neutral expression on his face; all his attention focussed upon Fiona.

"Why did you do that?" Njhay asked.

Fiona widened her eyes, cocked her head to one side. "Whatever do you mean?" she said.

"I *mean*, why did you knock her over?"

Fiona slipped a glance back at Alex, as if he might have some sort of an explanation, but Alex only shrugged by way of reply.

Louise felt the tension shred the air. She was the only one capable of diffusing it. "Really," she said. "It doesn't matter."

She felt pain sparking across her forehead and she reached up to rub her temples. It helped to mitigate the sensation somewhat, but she was still left with a low-level throb . . . by morning she could tell that she'd have a nasty-looking welt from where she'd fallen.

Apparently having regained her former bravado, Fiona took a stride forward, past Njhay and Louise. Alex trailed in her wake.

"Shouldn't you take her to the Infirmary?" Fiona said, treading out into the corridor. "Get her looked at?"

Louise felt Njhay's muscles tense as he held her, but, acting on instinct, she reached out and touched him on the chest, whispered, "*Don't...*"

Before any escalation could take place, the sound of Fiona and Alex's footsteps was disappearing off along the corridor as they headed for the refuge of their own suite.

Once Louise could no longer hear their footsteps, she couldn't help but blow out a long-held sigh.

Njhay, too, she sensed, allowed himself to relax slightly.

Only a second or so later did Louise recall that she was in Njhay's arms.

Her heart skipped a beat.

And, without thinking, she found herself staring back into his bronze-green eyes.

Although she was only dimly aware of their surroundings, she could sense the bleary starscape which stood behind them; all of the stars dotting the vast, unknown expanse of space. An infinity of possibilities opening out into the Evermore...

When she felt Njhay's arms loosening around her, she knew she had to take her chance.

Heart in mouth, she lurched forward into him and pressed her lips—*hard*—up against his. She breathed in the thick scent of musk and soil which clung to him, and she felt his rigid, rippling muscles up against her skin.

Thrills passed through her, over and over again.

She wasn't sure whether she could control herself.

Everything that had happened today made itself felt now.

She pushed her tongue into his mouth, feeling the rigid, smart lines of his teeth. She explored and explored until she found his tongue there, lying in the base of his mouth . . . *hiding* from her?

She gently eased it out of its lethargy.

Pressed it to her own.

She felt him take a profound breath, as if sucking her into him.

His gentle hands pressed into her thighs, and then, eased her upward, removing her feet from the floor. Before she knew quite what had happened, he held her in his arms—*carried* her in his arms.

Their lips parted.

And she found herself bathed in the bronze-green aeons of his eyes.

"We *could* get a doctor to look at that bump," he said. "But I thought I had the duty to let you know that I've got a few years of medical training . . . enough to deal with a bump on the head."

"Do you now?" Louise found herself saying, in a whimsical voice.

He smiled back at her. "A sordid detail from my past."

19

PASSION ENGAGED

Njhay carried her all the way to the PEAR landing strip. He went with her back to the Basements.

Louise was glad to have company . . . to *not* be alone.

On their way down to Louise's room, still carrying her in his arms, he picked up a bag of ice from the cafeteria. For this Louise was extremely grateful. As she lay in his arms, she held the bag to her head, savouring the cooling sensation, and the waylaying of the pain.

Njhay whisked Louise in through the doorway of her room. Then he lay her down on her bed.

Louise continued to press the bag of ice to her temple, feeling her own heartbeat in the fledgling lump. Her daze had left her, though. She felt clear-headed.

Njhay smiled. "You just lie back," he said, fluffing a pillow.

Louise allowed herself to sink. She felt better now. She took steady, cleansing breaths.

"Who *are* those two?" Njhay said, sitting on the edge of the bed and taking Louise's pulse.

For the first few seconds, Louise lost herself to his steady hold on her wrist; to those strong, rugged hands of his. And then she brought her attention back.

Picked out his bronze-green eyes . . . and those corkscrew curls which danced down the side of his face. Every so often, they proved such a nuisance that they had to be batted out of his eyes.

Louise really had no intention of getting into the intricacies of her relationship with Alex. And even less with getting into the details of her relationship with *Fiona*.

"Like you said," she replied. "Just some sordid detail from the past."

Thankfully, Njhay was kind enough to allow the matter to drop.

He leaned over her. "Just bring the ice away from your head for a second, okay?"

Louise did as he asked, unable to stop herself from smiling. It felt so surreal to see Njhay concentrating so hard on what was surely not a big issue.

"Okay," he said, "it's of my less-than-professional opinion that you'll live."

Almost moving apart from herself, she closed the gap on his thick, manly lips.

Pushed her body up against his.

This time, apparently prepared, he pushed back.

It seemed as if sparks tickled her veins. Her stomach clutched tight. The world seemed to dim. And then it returned to her . . . impossibly brightly.

She felt his hands fumbling for the zip at the back of her overalls.

And—*only a second or so later*—she realised she was doing the same.

Was this right?

Was this too fast?

... It didn't *feel* too fast ...

Freed from her overalls, she lay naked beneath him. The bag of ice was forgotten.

She absorbed his muscular, well-worked body.

His tanned, glistening skin.

And then, as it always seemed, she was dragged back to his unfathomable eyes.

She felt him enter her. Slowly. And impossibly warm.

She reached up, combed her fingers through those corkscrew curls.

Tugged lightly.

Felt his slight groan.

His steady, building thrusts.

Deeper and deeper ...

She met him.

Pushed him harder.

Urged him to thrust harder.

Her whole body seemed to float upward.

Incapable of being tethered down.

So long . . . it'd been so long since she'd felt like this . . . happy, passionate . . .

Loved.

She caught her darting thoughts.

A tingling sensation passed across the surface of her skin. Every hair seemed to stand to attention. Her whole body stiffened ... and then relaxed ...

His warm breath blew across her bare throat.

He lay on top of her—resting. Recharging.

His breath matched her own.

———

Louise awoke with a start.

For some reason she believed it was time to get up.

But, when she took in the display on the wall of her room, she saw that it was still very much the middle of the night beneath the Dome. She turned on her side, realising that she was still naked.

Njhay slept soundly, his corkscrew curls now all mussed; whatever measures he'd taken to tame his appearance for his meeting with Costatino ruined. He had laid his glasses down on the bedside table, apparently not needing them for the time being.

Louise rolled onto her back.

Stared up at the ceiling.

Her whole body was tingling . . . from head to toe.

When she reached up and felt for her forehead, she could feel the welt forming. A reminder of what had taken place earlier that evening. It was hard to equate the shove Fiona had given her with the same place—*the same time*—as what had happened later on.

Her past, her present, inextricably tied.

Unable to be parted.

"How's your concussion holding up?"

She turned to Njhay, seeing he had stirred from his sleep.

He wore a thick, satisfied smile.

"Like you said," she replied, "I think I'll live."

Njhay yawned widely, stifling it with the back of his hand. He breathed in deeply and then exhaled long and hard.

She watched as his entire body rippled and shifted with the

effect. He was like some kind of wild animal, barely tamed . . . held in check by those overalls, and that near ever-present lab coat.

She reached out and splayed her fingers over his chest.

Felt his heartbeat against her palm.

"So," she said, staring at a handsome freckle shrouded with rough, dark-brown hair just beneath his nipple, "did you take Schmoozing 101 while you were at medical school?"

"What'd you mean?" Njhay replied, smiling wider still.

"Tonight, with Costantino . . . you had him eating out of the palm of your hand."

"Oh, that . . ."

"I thought you couldn't stomach the business side of things here, beneath the Celestial Stays Dome; I thought that you'd gone out of your way to steer clear of it."

Njhay went quiet for a couple of moments, and Louise couldn't help wondering if she might've overstepped the mark. And yet, she couldn't help but feel at ease in his company.

Before he replied, he reached out for her hand, squeezed it. "Guess I'm just a walking bag of contradictions, huh?"

"Guess we all are, in a way."

There was a pause, and Louise, somehow, knew what was coming next.

"Who are those two—the woman who pushed you?"

This time, though, Louise knew just how to deal with the question.

With a flash of her eyebrows, she reached out and neatly shoved him onto his back.

She'd make him forget all about that push.

LUNAR TOURIST PROTOCOL

*S*ince *Louise's guests* had already seen the highlights of what the Moon had to offer, she found herself at something of a loose end as to what to treat her guests to next.

Thankfully, Mackenzie was on hand—or at least in her *ear*—to offer a ready-made itinerary.

Louise was to escort her guests to the Orbital Café that morning so that everybody could get their dose of caffeine, before venturing off across the lunar plains again for a grand tour of the Apollo 11 landing site. Mackenzie assured Louise that Miguel Cruz would lead proceedings in terms of the history; in terms of explaining the ins and outs of the exact details.

If Louise had learned anything at all about Costantino the day before, it was that he was a stickler for the *details* . . . he wanted to know the *how* and the *why* of everything. From what she had seen of Miguel Cruz so far, she could tell that he held the answers to innumerable questions.

Mackenzie saw fit to give her an assistant from Tourism for the day.

It was Kyra Singh, the recruit who had arrived the same day as Louise.

The two of them met in the cafeteria where they—*again*—shared a near-mute breakfast, despite Louise's best efforts to get Kyra to open up.

They caught a PEAR out to the Lunar Grand where they picked up their guests.

Louise wasn't too surprised to be informed by Costantino that Gofreddo wouldn't be joining them until a little later; that he was having trouble 'waking up'.

Unfortunately, the same couldn't be said for Alex and Fiona, who—like a pair of faithful dogs emotionally attached to Costantino's heels—arrived right on time.

Bereft of Gofreddo, they headed to the Orbital Café.

Louise supposed that the café had been modelled on an Alpine chalet, and although she couldn't help admitting that it was logically *wildly* out of place to be found here—on the lunar surface—in a strange way it *worked*.

It was painted in Christmas reds and greens. Wooden roof tiles and window frames which seemed—at least to Louise's inexpert eye—to have been handcrafted.

Perhaps it was because, back when she'd worked at Humble Associates, and she had had occasion to visit a chalet, it had been with a wild and wintry backdrop—the kind of conditions where warmth and comfort were at a premium . . . and where a chalet offered both of those things.

Alicia Brennan stood in the doorway, ready to greet them.

Louise supposed this measure wasn't quite standard protocol.

She couldn't help but notice the pair of earrings which Alicia wore; a golden sun hanging from each lobe. Before she got the chance to ask Alicia about them, Costantino clapped his hands together enthusiastically and let loose a chortle of pleasure. "Oh, *my dear*," he said. "Wonderful—*really* wonderful."

He looked to her, waiting for her to nod, giving him permission to reach out and touch the golden earrings. He glanced back at Louise—Alex and Fiona hanging nearby.

"This is the *Sol de Mayo*," he said, caressing one of the earrings. "One of the symbols of my country."

Costantino let go of the earring, allowing Alicia to straighten back into her normal posture. He pointed to her and grinned from ear to ear. "You, my dear—*you* are a wonder."

He glanced back to Alex and Fiona, ushering them inside.

Louise held back for a moment, aware that Kyra, too, was nearby. As Louise brushed past Alicia, she couldn't help but whisper, in her ear, "Excellent market research."

Alicia smiled back. "Excellent bed-work, from what I hear." She added a wink for good measure then indicated her forehead, clearly referencing the unsightly welt at Louise's temple. "A good night by all accounts."

Feeling self-conscious all of a sudden, Louise reached up for the welt and touched it lightly. She felt a sting. She flinched, then sucked at her teeth.

When she glanced to Kyra, she could tell, from her smirking expression, that she'd heard the news too. To begin with, Louise was a little knocked back . . . surprised at how fast news had spread of what she'd believed to be her *private* life.

And then she realised that here, on the Moon, gossip really was as fierce and quick-spreading as any small town worth its salt back on Earth . . .

Once inside the Orbital Café, Louise was almost knocked back by the warm, sweet smells. It was only now, about a week after she'd got up here, to the Moon, that she came to realise how much of a sugar junky she truly was . . . the cafeteria mainly fulfilled a necessity rather than indulging a sweet tooth.

The inside of the café maintained the consistency of the exterior, what with its wooden beams, and the cosy, animated open fireplace which gave off very realistic warmth. What was different, though, at least from all the chalets which Louise had visited, was the paraphernalia which hung from the walls; which hung down from the support beams.

Louise could recall a time when, on a business trip with Alex no less, the two of them had met up with some Swiss contacts in such a locale. The whole chalet had been decked out with all manner of vintage skis, snowshoes and—*most memorably*—a stuffed bear.

Here, though, there was no sign of anything to do with skiing.

Everything was space-travel paraphernalia.

An oxygen tank.

Several pieces of kit, with gauges and dials, which Louise really couldn't so much as *speculate* the use of. Then, just as there had been that stuffed bear in that chalet, there was a spacewalk suit standing up near the entrance of the café. Louise peered at her own reflection in the mercury-coloured visor. It sent a slight shudder about her collar. It was ghostly in the same way a suit of armour might be in an abandoned castle corridor.

A reminder of the past.

Rather than the modern, calming techno music which was so often employed throughout the Dome, the Orbital Café featured the burbling sounds of space communications; one piece of apparatus speaking to the other . . . the odd gushing jet of a thruster, or whatever that sound might denote.

It reminded Louise of one of those playlists which featured nothing but dolphin or whale calls.

And it was just as soothing.

Alicia had already set them a table near one of the windows, looking out across the lunar plains.

Louise wandered over to join the guests. She was deeply aware of Kyra clinging to her heels.

"What happened to your *head?*" Costantino asked, sitting across the table from her.

"Oh," Louise said, flushing slightly, and hoping that neither Fiona or Alex had overheard. "I walked into a door."

Costantino frowned. "But the doors here all *slide.*" As if to prove his point, he acted out the motion with his hands, drawing them together and then tearing them apart.

"Uh, it was . . ."—Louise trailed off for a second; her mind going truly blank—". . . *faulty.*"

Thankfully, Alicia arrived to take their order. Once done, she disappeared off into the kitchens.

Under any other circumstances, this might've meant a silence draping itself over the table like an unpleasant, damp sheet. However, this particular *circumstance* involved Costantino Zito.

A man driven by curiosity and *vitality.*

"So," he said, clutching his hands before him on the table, and staring across at Louise. "Tell me all about your past involvement with Humble."

Louise stalled as best as she could.

She flashed several glances in Alex and Fiona's direction, hoping that one of them might take up the mantel of answering Costantino's question . . . but both avoided her gaze.

She even shifted a sidelong glance at Kyra, as if she might be able to aid her.

But she was clearly just as curious as Costantino was.

"I . . . uh," Louise began, unconvincingly. "I used to serve as Public Relations Manager."

Costantino pouted, tilting his head to one side.

She had no idea what Alex had already said about her; if he had even admitted that she had worked for him. As far as she knew, she might be treading heavily on his toes; exposing his lies.

But, then again, that was his prerogative. She could only tell the truth from her perspective. She could only do what was good for her.

And her *future*.

Sensing a pause in the conversation, Costantino put in, "And why did you decide to leave?" He smiled that winning smile of his, laughter lines creasing the sides of his face.

It was a smile which relieved tension whatever the circumstance.

And Louise was glad for it now.

It convinced her that what she was doing—what she was *saying* —was right.

It was the *only* thing she could say.

"I wanted to, ah . . . *travel*," Louise finally replied. And then, trying out a smile, added, "To come to the Moon."

"Uh-huh," Costantino said, still smiling to himself; but with his eyes wandering now, searching out Alex's eyes.

Louise was *certain* she had put her foot in it now.

"All-righty."

The whole table turned its attention to Alicia, standing over them, bearing crafted wicker trays with their orders sitting on top.

For a second, Louise lost herself in the freshly baked scents of the apple strudels, the Bakewell tarts, the pain au chocolat, and the blueberry muffins. And all of it brought together by the smell of the cups of tea and coffee smouldering away alongside.

Apparently noting the sense of unease which clouded the table like a thick fog, Alicia went about her work quickly and efficiently, pausing only when she straightened up to flash a wide smile at Costantino. "Enjoy," she stated, simply.

Louise watched on as she left, observing one of her gold earrings catching the light playfully.

Louise would've given just about anything to be in Alicia's shoes—to not be charged with entertaining one of the most successful men in the history of the world . . . and stay on cool, pleasant—*formal*—terms with an ex-boyfriend.

Once Alicia had disappeared behind the counter, retreating to her baking, Louise pressed herself back into action. But when she looked across the table at Costantino she saw that he was now distracted by the baked goods which had appeared before him.

She could tell, from the look of his expression, that he was as much of an admirer of good cooking as he was of human endeavour.

It was then, as Louise blew across the surface of her smouldering coffee and eyed up one of the pain au chocolat with malicious intent that she noticed Fiona rising up out of her seat, and, smartly, weaving her way through the empty tables and chairs surrounding.

Louise studied her path. She came to the conclusion—soon enough—that she was in distress.

With a heavy heart, Louise left the baked goods behind, excusing herself from the table.

She hoped Kyra would hold the fort.

In the women's toilets, the same space soundtrack played out. She probably used the same technique Wendy had put into action to locate her intended target . . . she searched for the cubicle with the closed door. The feet showing in the gap beneath.

It was only as Louise stood outside the door, ready to bring her knuckles down against the wood to alert the occupant, that she heard a *sniffle* from within.

It caught her off-guard.

She was unsure what she should do.

Could she still back out?

Pretend nothing had happened?

But, surely, Fiona had heard her footfall . . .

It would be cowardly to back out now; and Louise was through with being a coward.

"Fiona?" Louise said.

She waited for the reply.

"Are you okay in there?"

Another *sniff*.

Followed by a nose-blow.

". . . Fine, thanks," came the response.

Louise held her ground, knowing that now wasn't a time to back out. "Is everything all right? Is there anything I can help with . . . I know how lunar life can be a bit bumpy . . ."

Listen to her, sounding as if she was a veteran, barely a week into her service.

"It's just . . ." Fiona replied ". . . I've heard stories—the things that people *say*."

"About Alex?"

137

"About Alex . . ."

Louise drew a deep breath.

It was hard to believe that she was having this conversation.

How she, Alex's ex-girlfriend . . . his ex-'business partner' . . . whatever it was she had been, was now thick in conversation with his current one.

And that, for the most part, the tone of their interaction was courteous.

"What"—Fiona snorted into a tissue—"*happened*, exactly?"

Louise reached up, touched the welt on her forehead . . . the one which Fiona had dealt her the previous night. She wondered if she should tell the truth . . . somebody had been kind enough to tell *her* the truth once . . . to tell her that which she had refused to hear—or *see*—for so long.

"I realised," Louise said, "that everything I'd achieved—that everything *good* that'd happened to me at Humble, was all down to Alex . . . that it was because I was . . ."

Here she felt the tears welling in her eyes; and a shudder ran down her spine . . . wow, how she really *didn't* want to be going into these places, and yet, look at her . . .

". . . Alex was putting everything into place for me—*doing* everything for me; and I realised that . . . I realised that he was, in a way, *rewarding* me for being his girlfriend . . . presenting me with this lifestyle, with this *job* that just . . . well, it simply *wasn't* mine . . ."

Fiona said nothing in reply. Louise realised she was waiting for her to continue.

So Louise did.

"I couldn't help thinking Alex would treat anybody as he'd treated me; that all the *perks* he'd granted me were bribes; a means for him to keep me. And so, one day . . . one day . . ." Louise had to catch herself before her voice broke. "So that one day he would be able to say to me, 'Look—*look*—at everything I've given you . . . it's *all* because of me.'"

Louise shook her head to herself, unsure whether or not she was getting through. Maybe she was just rambling. Maybe she was exposing herself as some borderline lunatic.

But she had told the truth.

She had done *that*, at least.

"I had to run," Louise said. "It was the only way—the only way out I could see."

There was a long, long pause in the women's toilets.

"Just one question," Louise continued. "I just have one more question for you, if it's okay?"

Louise half expected Kyra or Alicia to appear in the doorway; for one or the other to break up this apparently joyous little meeting of minds; that standard setup of one woman locked inside the cubicle; another on the outside, coaxing her out.

But neither appeared.

Louise turned back to the cubicle door. "Did Alex . . . *does* Alex ever get angry . . . you know what I mean . . . does he get out of control?"

A longer, yawning pause.

A *sniffle* . . .

Could it be assent?

Or was it just coincidence?

Finally, from within the cubicle, the toilet flushed.

Another sniffle and the door creaked open on its hinges.

Fiona stood before Louise, in the doorway.

Her eyes were mucky with makeup. There were a couple of dark stains from where her mascara had dripped and fallen onto the front of her visitors' overalls.

Fiona just stood still, staring Louise down.

"I'm sorry," Fiona said. "*So* sorry about yesterday—about pushing you. It's just . . . when I demanded an explanation from Alex, about who you were, he told me the truth; or, I *thought* he told me the truth . . . I was angry." Her eyes instinctively drifted up to the spot on Louise's forehead. "I was an *idiot*."

"Come on," Louise said, with a slight smile. "Let's make you presentable."

As the two of them left the toilets behind, Louise wondered if Fiona might lie to herself about Alex; just as Louise had to *herself* for such a long time.

Sooner or later, though, she would need to face the truth.

Just as Louise had done.

LEAVE OF ABSENCE

ouise was glad when Mackenzie relieved her of the group of guests the next day, assigning them to Wendy. As the two of them strode through the Crescent Gardens, a few days later, the plants all still glowing with whatever magic Njhay had dealt them, Louise was sure to notice Mackenzie's unpanicked, almost laid-back manner. So different from the image she had built up of Mackenzie from the first time they had met; the ferocious, cold figure stuffing that finger of hers into her inner-ear at any moment of her choosing.

Mackenzie asked for an explanation of the welt on Louise's forehead, and she explained it away as being a souvenir of the Shuttle ride they'd taken to the Apollo 11 landing site . . . that Patrick Fourie—their pilot for the day—had taken certain liberties.

Louise wasn't convinced that it'd been *totally* necessary for him to dive into so many craters; or to commit so many loop-the-loops.

When Mackenzie slipped her a sidelong glance, Louise was

surprised to see that she was smiling . . . and that her cheeks were slightly flushed. "Well, unfortunate dings aside, you have no idea, blue eyes. No idea at all."

"About what?"

"About just how *pleased* Costantino is with you—about the *hospitality* he's received thus far in his visit."

"Well," Louise said, feeling a touch embarrassed. "I'm sure it's all down to the team."

"You know, I didn't want to say anything about it before, but there's quite a great deal riding on Costantino's visit—this isn't exactly a *recreational* trip as I might've had you believe."

"Oh?" Louise replied, not feeling entirely surprised.

Wherever a businessman of Costantino's stature was involved she was certain that there was always an ulterior motive lying just around the corner.

Mackenzie nodded along with herself. "Yes, you see, the higher-ups—which is to say, *my* higher-up—Karolin Köhler, has been in discussion with Costantino; to close an advertising deal."

Louise, of course—having carried out her due-diligence before accepting the job offer—knew just who Karolin Köhler was. No less than the managing director of Celestial Stays . . . head honcho, top cat . . . or whatever phrase came to mind.

It took Louise slightly aback to think that Mackenzie had the ear of Frau Köhler . . . even though she'd spent the past forty-eight hours in the company of Costantino Zito . . .

Mackenzie drew in a deep breath. "As with all things, Costantino can be a stubborn old mule."

Louise blinked a couple of times—unable to get her head around *this* comparison. From everything she'd seen of him so far, she couldn't say that he was anything but charming.

But, then again, she supposed a hardened businessman such as

Costantino Zito hadn't got as far as he had solely on sunshine and smiles.

Mackenzie went on, "Likes to see what it is he's selling before he's prepared to sell it himself, if you see what I mean?"

Realising that they'd trod all their way to one of the outer limits of the Crescent Gardens—and that they'd run out of footpath—Louise came to a standstill.

Mackenzie soon aped her.

"What's he looking for?" Louise said, meeting Mackenzie's brilliant green eyes.

Mackenzie shrugged, flashed a smile.

Behind that smile, though, Louise could sense a touch of anxiety.

"Who knows?" Mackenzie replied. "This is the first time Frau Köhler has had dealings with Costantino. But from the stories that are frequently bandied about, it can be so much as a single detail which throws him off—which causes him to scrap a prospective deal."

Louise felt a ticklish sensation pass through her blood.

While she'd been on edge before—while offering Costantino the very best hospitality she could manage—she had eased herself into the task; and, dare she say it, become *comfortable.*

Now, though, she knew that a fresh tension would enter her interactions with Costantino.

And Louise couldn't help but wonder if this had been Mackenzie's true intention.

It was difficult to forget what Njhay had said—about Mackenzie doing her best to take down anybody who might be considered a threat.

"So," Louise replied, finally. "What you're saying is that you want me to spy on him?"

Mackenzie narrowed an eye. "Not *spy* on him, but I'd like you to let me know about anything you notice—any *throwaway* comments; any *askance* looks."

Louise wasn't certain how what she asked couldn't be considered spying . . .

"I'll see what I can do."

"Good," Mackenzie said, with a smile, finally thrusting her finger into her ear for the first time in their entire exchange. "I'll be in touch when you're back on duty tomorrow morning."

It wasn't planned—*per se*—but Louise found herself drifting about the Crescent Gardens lab hallways. Once she was there, it only made sense to drop in on Njhay.

As always when Louise peered in through the doorway, she saw that he was stooped over his microscope, conducting a study of this, that or the other.

"Knock, knock," she said.

Just as he had done the first day they'd met, he straightened up suddenly, dinging his head on the pipe which jutted out of the ceiling. He let out a howl. Louise restrained the urge to laugh. She was glad to see that he'd safely discarded his glasses to one of the metal examination tables before getting to grips with his microscope.

Rubbing at his pained scalp, Njhay turned to her, pinning on a smile.

Today Louise could see that his hair had already initiated the fightback against the attempted taming which'd taken place ahead of the grand demonstration a couple of nights before.

As always—as Louise had always *seen* him—his lab coat was a little bedraggled while the overalls he wore underneath were hardly much better.

He stepped toward her, his hurting scalp apparently forgotten. He squinted as he drew close, his attention focussed on her forehead. He winced. "Wow," he said, "that really is a *shiner* . . ."

Louise flashed her eyes at him by way of reply. "Yeah, and it seems to be just about the only thing anybody can talk about today."

Leaning in closer, he narrowed his eyes even further. "Did you put any ice on it last night?"

Louise gave a ditsy, open-mouthed expression, pressing her index finger into the pit of her chin. "Guess I forgot—there wasn't any clever medical man to be had."

To tell the truth, Louise had been so exhausted following the previous day that she *had* clean forgotten about the welt. It had been the last thing on her mind when—*feet aching; brain pleading for sleep*—she'd allowed herself to slump down on her bed.

Louise drew back from him. "You weren't *lonely*, were you?"

The corners of Njhay's mouth tweaked back. "Nah," he replied. "Why would I be *lonely*?"

She took a few steps away from him, over to the panel which glowed out of thin air; thick with graphs, and statistics, and all manner of data. "What does all this *mean*?" she found herself saying. "All of these colours . . . all of these numbers; *percentages*?"

As Louise stood at one of the displays, she felt Njhay coming up behind her, as she had imagined in so many fantasies which'd played out in her mind throughout the past week . . . throughout the past twenty-four hours while they'd been apart.

"Well," Njhay said, placing his arms steadily on her shoulders. "You need to have spent an *awfully* long time at university to even begin to fathom."

Louise continued to stare at the displays as she felt Njhay's hands wandering their way up the sides of her neck; as she felt his mouth pucker and brush her skin. His breath was warm—*minty fresh*. She breathed in his musky scent, tapered by the lightest dab of cologne.

It was too much for her to bear.

She turned in his arms.

The tips of their noses almost touched.

She stared into his bronze-green eyes . . . like some undiscovered precious metal.

"You know," Njhay said, with a wide smile, "it's a long time since I've been this happy." He paused then added, "Since I've been able to *trust* again."

Louise held his gaze, wondering whether she should pick up on what Njhay had just said. But there was some block; something which kept her from asking a follow-up question, because she knew that it would lead to questions about her past . . . and she wanted to leave the past behind her.

Where it belonged.

She reached out for his hand, squeezed it. "Any plans for this afternoon?"

Njhay glanced about him, to the lab. His expression creased a little, and Louise knew that he had other things on his mind—things *other* than their fledgling relationship. And yet, the feeling came out of nowhere. A sense of hurt. A sense of *injustice*.

Was it that word . . . so simple a thing as Njhay *uttering* that word?

. . . Trust . . .

She couldn't help but wonder if she might be setting herself up for the same fall she had suffered at Alex's hand. Could she really trust anyone ever again?

Could she really *love* anyone ever again?

When he turned back to her, she was ready.

"It's okay," she said. "I shouldn't have come here—not while you're working." She took another few steps back, so he wouldn't be able to reach out and touch her. "Maybe," she continued, holding onto that word for a long while. "Maybe *later*," she finished, finally.

As she trod away, she already heard him coming after her. She could tell that he was *pursuing* her . . . and yet she knew that she needed to leave him behind; that she needed to leave him to his work.

She had no way of knowing his mind—of knowing the mind of a scientist.

She couldn't help but think just how long Njhay would be around from now on; surely he had his own plans. Surely the situation here—this careful balancing of science and commerce—would get to him eventually. He would feel compelled to leave.

There could be no other way.

As she passed through the doorway, she felt a single tear break free from the corner of her eye. It streaked down her cheek. And one thought remained sketched on her mind—one thought *only* . . .

Never again.

22

DISTANCE

hroughout the day's activities—their *second* full day on the Moon—Alex couldn't help but notice that Fiona had grown distant with him; that she was avoiding his gaze, doing her best not to speak with him unless entirely necessary.

It should've been the perfect day.

Once again, Costantino's son—Gofreddo—had ducked out of the day's activities.

This meant that, except for the Celestial Stays employee they were burdened with—a lady in her fifties called Wendy—Alex had the perfect opportunity to chew over future business plans with none other than Costantino himself. Or 'Tino', as he was supposed to call him.

However, Fiona's manner was proving a distraction. Alex would've liked nothing else than to be alone with her for a matter of minutes so that he might thrash out whatever it was that was troubling her; so that he might illuminate the way ahead.

It'd been so strange that he'd found himself sharing the same space with Louise . . . when he'd so thoroughly believed that she'd gone for good . . . and after all that he'd *given* her . . . after he had made a *life* for her. And yet, despite knowing how she'd hurt him, he couldn't help but feel that old, familiar thrill at the base of his gut. Call it love, or affection, or even just plain *nostalgia* . . . but it was there. And it bothered him immensely.

At the entrance to the Lunar Caverns, the Celestial Stays employee—Wendy—oversaw each of them putting on their protective gear; plastic hats all around, along with an emergency oxygen mask and tank. Wendy reasoned that—despite them being in the Dome—if there was a failure in some of the atmospheric systems, the backup measures might not be strong or far-reaching enough to flood the Caverns with the oxygen they needed to breathe.

Alex had always had a thing about enclosed, confined spaces— the trip from Earth had been somewhat nerve-rankling—so he couldn't say he was thrilled about the arrangement.

Still, they pressed on all the same, with Costantino grinning from ear to ear.

That was the most important thing.

To keep the *big* man happy.

In truth, Alex was still absorbing just what an enormously significant opportunity this was. And not just *personally*, but for the whole of Humble Associates.

Costantino was what was known as a 'king-maker' within the business world . . . he had the ability to take whatever Alex and his partners might be planning to the next level.

Alex glanced over his shoulder—to Fiona, skulking along behind.

He flashed her a look, but, again, she averted his gaze.

What *was* it? What was her problem?

He thought back to the Stellar Tide Casino, when she had accidentally-on-purpose knocked Louise over; near enough flattened her nose. She had shown some pep there. Some *spirit*.

He knew from experience that scorned lovers were a tricky business, especially when placed in 'emotional' circumstances such as these ...

Deciding to disregard Fiona for the time being, Alex strode on ahead, catching up with Costantino. The two of them paced through the Lunar Caverns while Wendy—*up ahead*—pointed out various geological features which, quite honestly, Alex couldn't have given two shits about.

Once Wendy had—*finally*—shut up for the foreseeable future, he turned his attention onto Costantino; catching his eye. "So," he said, putting on a broad grin, "the Menthol Grill, hmm?"

Costantino seemed lost for a few moments. His gaze drifted away from Alex's, and back onto Fiona. Then he pressed on a smile. The distinctive, hearty tone of his voice gave Alex a pleasing, warming feeling in his gut. "Yes," Costantino replied, "a most wonderful appliance."

Still smiling, Alex continued, "I was just wondering about it, actually, about where an appliance such as that one might go with the approval of a man such as yourself—what sorts of ..."

But Costantino stopped Alex, holding up his palm. "Excuse me for perhaps sounding discourteous, but maybe you should speak with your wife? She does not seem to be feeling very well, I think, or, ah, maybe she is not happy about something?"

Alex couldn't help himself—couldn't *control* himself.

He wrestled not to correct Costantino's assumption that Fiona was his wife.

He flashed a glare at her.

Like a faithful pedigree *dog*, she picked her way carefully through the Moon rock while following at a safe distance.

Before he had a chance to recover—to come up with some sort of explanation—Costantino had clapped him on the shoulder in a fatherly manner and stridden onward; deeper into the Caverns, after their leader, Wendy.

Alex crunched his fingers into fists and waited for Fiona.

When she came up alongside him, she tried to sidle past, again without meeting his eye.

He reached out, grabbed hold of her wrists.

Wrestled her into his chest.

Through gritted teeth, he said, "What? What *is* it? What's *bothering* you?"

Her eyes widened. Her lips parted slightly. It reminded him so much of those times when he had grabbed hold of Louise whenever she was getting out of line.

Fiona opened her mouth to respond, but no sound emanated from within.

He kept his voice low so neither Costantino or Wendy—*but mostly Costantino*—wouldn't overhear. "You *do* realise how important this is for me—how important it is for *us*? For *Humble*?"

Fiona stared back at him, long and hard. "I want to know the answer to a question."

Unable to believe what he was hearing, Alex blinked rapidly as if he might rid himself of a daze. "I'm sorry, *what?*"

"I need an answer."

Still stunned, Alex stared at her.

"If it came to your job"—he noticed Fiona swallow; *hard*—"and *me*, which one would you choose?"

" 'Which would I choose' ?"

Fiona nodded.

A giddiness struck him. He wasn't sure he could handle it—that he could *control* it. Soon enough, he was laughing. Finally, he drew a deep breath, down to the pit of his gut.

And he eyeballed Fiona.

"Which one do you *think* I'd choose?"

She pressed her lips tightly together.

Neither one of them said anything.

But they both knew the answer.

23

RECONCILIATION

rapped in a towel, with the odour of a thick, lemony perfume all around, Louise's earpiece informed her that there was somebody at the door of her room. She paused, glanced about her, into the steam which continued to emanate from the bathroom.

When she did a quick check, she still had twelve hours or so before she went back on duty.

If she wasn't mistaken, she had set her status to Do Not Disturb.

Perhaps the Link wasn't as fool-proof as Celestial Stays's reputation for quality seemed to imply.

With a long, satisfying sigh, she breathed out her frustration and ordered her room door to slide open. Standing there, in the gap, was Njhay. He had shucked his lab coat—as any half-decent scientist wary of cross-contamination might've done—and he looked quite simple in his royal-blue, Celestial Stays overalls.

He almost looked like *just another employee*.

As if, just like the rest of them, he was here to do a job.

"Hi," he began.

It wasn't the strongest of starts but Louise was taken enough by his appearance to reply, "And what brings you to my bedchamber?"

"Well," Njhay replied, with a slight smile, reaching an arm up to lean his weight up against the doorframe, "I was wondering if I could take you out."

" 'Take me out' ?" Louise replied, widening her eyes. "Where do you intend to *take me out* to?"

Njhay shrugged, and then, with mock surprise and a smart snap of his fingers, he leaped into action. "Hang on," he said. "Think I've got just the place."

"Where?" Louise said, a little annoyed with herself for so blatantly expressing her interest.

"Have you been to the Lunar Caverns yet?"

Louise shook her head. "No, they haven't cropped up on my itinerary."

"So, what do you say?"

Louise held back, knowing that she needed to keep her cards a little closer to her chest. That she needed to play just a little coy. "Well, I *am* washing my hair tonight."

Njhay brought his arm away from where he rested it against the doorframe. His smile—once brilliant—faded a touch.

Louise felt a slight victory at this. "I wouldn't want you to miss out on any *important* discoveries because you were taking some non-entity like me out to some *stupid* Lunar Caverns . . ."

She allowed her words to tail off, and waited for Njhay's reaction—hoping he might take the bait. But, it seemed, he was wily to her games.

With a sly smile, he waggled a finger at her, then stepped away from the doorway. "I'll catch us a PEAR, shall I?" As he slipped from sight, trudging off along the corridor, she heard him add, over his shoulder, "Ten minutes—don't be late."

As she ordered her bedroom door shut, she stared at her reflection in the mirror—the current setting which occupied the wallpaper. She stared long and hard into her own eyes.

Could she see a warning there?

Was this just a flash in the pan?

Or was it the real thing?

On the way to the Lunar Caverns, Louise expected Njhay to get fresh with her; to at least go for the old—*old*—trick of pretending to yawn so that he could put his arm around her shoulders.

But, as it turned out, he was the perfect gentleman.

As they swerved through the air of the Dome, headed over the chalk-white lights of the buildings and pathways down below, Louise had to pinch herself to prove she wasn't dreaming every last detail. She was really here—on the Moon—and with such a *fetching* man . . .

The PEAR slowed as it descended, bringing them in on quite a steep trajectory. Louise felt her stomach sink. She couldn't help but feel that—despite the significantly slower speed of the PEAR— she'd been rendered slightly traumatised by the experience of the lunar Shuttle, bombing it across the plains to the Apollo 11 landing site.

It would be a while longer till she had any ideas about striving out across the lunar plains once again . . . then again, since she was contracted to Celestial Stays, she supposed she might not get to make that decision. If they told her to go, she would have no option.

The Lunar Caverns themselves were illuminated with a series of blinking orange lights. It reminded Louise of a time when—*on a business trip*—she and Alex had taken a stopover in Singapore. Jetlagged and feeling as if they'd landed on another planet, they'd stumbled about the streets, getting lost, until they'd finally come across a neat pond with a traditional Chinese-style house sitting on the water. There had been ceremonial, engraved stone statues about the periphery too. But it had been the pretty, tangerine tea lights which'd really given it a magical sparkle—which'd made it seem as if it wasn't quite real.

She could still recall the feeling as Alex had wrapped his arms about her from behind, as he had gently rested his chin on her shoulder and how the two of them had seemed to stare at the sight for such a long time. Until they'd both received a reminder that they had to return to the airport.

As always, it had been the Link which'd broken the magic of reality.

Like the gentleman he was—or at least the gentleman he was painting himself to be—Njhay hopped out of the PEAR first and then offered his hand to her. She accepted, and allowed him to lower her down onto the ground outside the transport.

As if respecting their privacy, the PEAR brought its visor shut, and took off into the air once more. The two of them watched it duck and weave as it headed back along its programmed trajectory; off to go and pick up more passengers.

When Louise turned back, she saw that Njhay was staring at her.

And she almost lost herself in his eyes once more.

"This way," Njhay said, taking hold of her hand, and leading her toward the mouth of the Lunar Caverns, illuminated with orange tea lights.

The Caverns themselves were lit up with the more standard milky-white Dome lights, making it so the eye could easily make out any of the obstacles within; so that they could avoid any unpleasant stumbles. As Louise took in the crooked, sponge-like roof of the cave, she wondered if they should have brought hard hats with them. She had always been a stickler for safety equipment, as if a helmet would be able to save them if there was a cave-in, or something similar.

After walking for about five minutes, they reached a Y-junction.

One side was illuminated.

The other was set in darkness.

Njhay simply turned to Louise, smiled, and said, "Do you trust me?"

It surely took Louise longer to respond than Njhay anticipated.

In the end, Louise nodded in reply.

Njhay reached down into his overalls and produced a pair of illumination sticks. He handed one of them to her. She took it from him.

With a twist, they turned both of them on with a brief flicker.

Cool, blue light illuminated their surroundings.

Peering into the darkened tunnel ahead, Njhay said, "According to Wendy, they'll have this fork all lit up by the end of the month."

"Well, that'll be no fun," Louise said, twisting her neck to look into the depths of the darkness. "How will people break their necks?"

Njhay chuckled and led them onward.

It took another ten minutes of walking—though at a much slower pace than they'd managed in the better-illuminated portion of the Caverns—before Louise noticed, up ahead, the orange tea lights again. She reached out for the back of Njhay's overalls and gave them a tug. "I thought you said this fork wouldn't be lit up for another month."

He grinned back at her. "I lied."

Louise had only a few seconds to reflect on this statement before Njhay reached for her hand, squeezed it with his own, and pulled her on through the tunnel.

The two of them walked onward. A few times, Louise's scalp brushed the ceiling of the cave and she had vague worries about becoming decapitated.

Thankfully, though, she escaped harm.

Finally, they reached the source of the orange tea lights; a dugout circular portion of the Caverns. She took in the mattress lying in the centre; candles flickering all around it. Her gaze focussed in on the rose petals scattered about her feet, as if a lunar breeze had blown them there.

Speechless for a moment, she felt Njhay squeeze her hand tightly. "I know what you're thinking about the candles," he said, "that they might not be the best choice in an oxygen-rich environment." His smile widened. "But I can assure you that they're not just any candles—not like the ones you're accustomed to down on Earth . . ."

"*You* created them?"

Njhay made as if to nod and then arrested the gesture. "Well, actually, I've got this friend Earthside who was able to hook me up."

Louise arched an eyebrow. "And you didn't think it was a touch presumptive to bring candles up with you to the Dome? How did you know that there would be romance in the air?" She paused a second, and then added, "How can you be sure there's romance in the air *now?*"

Njhay flushed at this remark. His eyes averted hers. He scoped out the room, as if running through a mental checklist of the contents. "You could call it a hunch, I guess," he finally replied, then looked back at her. *"Is* there romance in the air?"

Louise held herself very still, enjoying these moments where she was making him suffer. One of the strongest weapons a woman possessed was that which caused male suffering.

She had learned that much in the course of her romantic life.

She reached out for him, her hand making for his muscular chest. "Why don't you tell me?"

Njhay flushed a touch deeper. And then he took her hand. Held it in hers.

He eased her down gently onto the mattress.

His hands were careful, as if she was a delicate piece of lab apparatus. Was he showing her that he valued her as much as he valued his work?

Was he showing her that which Alex had failed to?

They remained in their overalls for the longest time.

Louise couldn't help but feel a flashback to being a teenager come on; to when she would arrive home, in the early hours, with her boyfriend at the time. How they would—*ever so quietly*—sneak into the back garden of her home and kiss in the moonlight.

Well, now she had gone one better . . . she was on the Moon.

It had been a sweet relationship in many ways; how they had never progressed beyond the holding of hands, or those sensitive —ever-so *delicious*—kisses.

Both of them had remained clothed throughout . . .

Louise had taken it upon herself to end it, deciding that—with the university years still ahead of them—she hadn't the emotional resources to see out a long-term relationship.

This time it was Louise who reached up for the zipper on Njhay's overalls. She felt the metal clasp with her fingers and—*ever so slowly*—eased it gently down the teeth, bringing the join open in simple, careful phases. Soon, she had slipped his overalls down his *tightly packed* body.

She took in his hazelnut-coloured skin in the orange tea lights, and she couldn't help but reach out to touch him. Her heart beat up in her mouth. Her throbbing pulse sounded in her eardrums.

She surprised even herself when she leaned into him and bit his shoulder.

With a gasp, Njhay retreated from her slightly.

But Louise clung on.

He couldn't have it all his own way.

He had submitted to her now.

Although he tried to hold back, she overpowered him, dragging him down onto her still-clothed body. She felt his hardness up against him, and, on instinct, reached for him; took him in her hand.

Felt his warm breath against her skin.

His low groan against her ear.

When she felt all his muscles drawing tight—when she heard that snatching for breath at the back of his throat—she released him.

He bore down on her.

Those bronze-green eyes flashed with a fire previously unseen . . . at least by Louise.

Njhay lowered his lips down to her ear. "Now it's my turn," he said.

And Louise had no intention of running.

Louise stared up at the jagged rock above her head. She traced the lines, observing how this was a perfectly dug-out little cave. As her eyes continued to search, she unconsciously focussed on the small hole, about halfway up the wall, and perhaps large enough for a person to wriggle their way through. It made her think about life on the Moon . . . could something have once inhabited this place? Could it have used these caves to hide out; to squeeze its way through?

She lay back on the mattress, feeling Njhay's pleasantly warm, pleasantly moist—pleasantly *naked*—form alongside her.

What a delicious hunk of *meat* he'd turned out to be.

The gentle twinkling of the orange tea lights sent shudders across the surface of her skin. She supposed she had always imagined a romantic gesture such as this one . . . well, okay, she'd never thought that it would take place on the Moon; but she had often wondered if a boy—a *man*—would be sufficiently taken with her to put on something like this. And now she had her answer.

It was something which Alex Barn certainly never would've thought to lay on for her. Exactly *what* had she been thinking? What had she been *thinking* to have stayed so long with him?

. . . And what must Fiona be thinking right now?

With that thought on her mind, she heard a *clunk* at the end of the tunnel.

It was followed by a murmuring voice.

Njhay startled. He sat up straight. Reached about him for his glasses.

Finding them, he thrust them down across the bridge of his nose.

He peered out into the darkness.

"Not expecting company?" Louise said, feeling a mixture of giddiness and exhilaration.

Before Njhay so much as replied, he pulled her to her feet.

Still dazed from the lengthy love-making session, Louise's legs were gripped with a pins-and-needles sensation. She nearly lost her balance a couple of times. When she shifted her attention over to Njhay, she saw that he was hurriedly stepping into his overalls.

It took Louise another moment—another sound off along the tunnel—to realise that she should do the same.

Just about dressed, Njhay busied himself blowing out the tea lights surrounding the mattress. Unable to sustain a girlish giggle, Louise whispered, "What? What's the *matter*? Aren't we *allowed* to be here?"

But Njhay didn't seem in any mood for humour.

As the final tea light was extinguished, he remained straight-faced, staring off into the darkness of the tunnel they had passed through together.

"No," he finally answered.

Louise held herself still, unable to take any of this seriously. Not really. It was all like being back at school. Nothing was *really* playing out in the real world . . . there weren't the *real-world* consequences here.

Footsteps continued to approach them, Louise's dizzy smile deserted her for the first time. Her heart thumped against her ribs as the danger—as the *implications*—of what sort of trouble they might get into fully struck her.

Could they get fired for this?

"Hello?" came the voice from out of the darkness.

It took Louise a couple of heartbeats to realise who it was. *Wendy*.

She was of half a mind to call out to her; to tell her that she and

Njhay were here. That it was *just* them . . . but then she snapped back to reality; reminded herself that Wendy was their superior . . . a *Guardian* . . . and although Louise herself had been made a Guardian—at least for the days of Costantino Zito's visit—she knew that it wouldn't be enough for her to pull rank; to pull any sort of privilege, over Wendy.

As though in agreement with her thoughts, she felt Njhay reach out from the darkness. His hand grasped hold of her shoulder. Squeezed.

She was in no doubt over what it meant.

That she was to be quiet.

Finally—*surely inevitably*—a light blinked on.

Lit up their surroundings.

That same, cool, blue light from the illumination sticks.

Unable to stop herself, Louise reached up and blocked the glare with her forearm.

"Well, well, well," came Wendy's voice from behind the near-blinding light. "Who've we got here—what've we got *going on* here?"

Not having grown accustomed to the sudden brightness, and yet unwilling to take any kind of reprimand lying down, Louise spoke up. "Just taking an afterhours stroll in the Caverns."

Even as those words made it out through her lips, Louise knew that she was out of line; that she would only bring on more problems for the two of them.

Wendy, though, didn't sound angry when she spoke again.

In fact, the most alarming thing—*at least for Louise*—was that she didn't seem to address either of them at all.

"As you can see," she said, "here at Celestial Stays, we put as much emphasis on our employees' enjoyment as that of our guests."

From out of darkness, Louise heard a hearty *chuckle*.

One which she recognised instantly.

Her eyes having got used to the light now, she peered beyond Wendy, over her shoulder, to the figure standing there.

Costantino Zito.

Her heart hung in her throat. She thought about what Mackenzie had told her . . . how it could be so much as the smallest slip which could cost Celestial Stays his business; and, already, she knew, she'd messed it up.

Beyond him, though, those other figures standing at his heels.

Although her brain told her that it could be no one else, the fact that her eyes hadn't yet adjusted sufficiently to make out their facial features left her in suspense. She prayed that it would be anyone else, that—*somehow*—in the past twenty-four hours while Louise hadn't been on duty, Costantino had grouped with somebody else.

But, as she could slowly observe now, she knew she was only deceiving herself.

Fiona Adams.

Alex Barn.

Their eyes were wide.

And they were focussed on her.

Louise drew a deep, shuddering breath, and then glanced back to Njhay.

What would happen to them now?

24

REPRIMAND

*I*t was a long time since Njhay had felt as if he'd got himself into some kind of deep trouble, but this was one of those times. He had been instructed to return to his room in the Basements—to get some rest—and then report for duty as usual in the morning.

And that was what he'd done.

As he stood in the lab—what he'd so often considered to be some sort of refuge within the Celestial Stays Dome—he felt himself trembling all over. Of course, that morning, he hadn't been able to concentrate on his work; he had been distracted by what he knew was coming. He knew he'd done wrong, and that there was nothing he could do to rectify his error . . .

Outside the lab, he could hear footsteps approaching. He was certain that it would be Mackenzie Angliss, and that, with that easy—*satisfied*—smirk she would deliver the news that he had been waiting for . . . that he was to be dismissed from his duties immediately.

As he paced back and forth, he couldn't help but imagine how long she'd waited for an opportunity such as this one. It would be such a clean-cut case. Although, on better days, he might've liked to see himself as being somewhat apart from the other operations of the Celestial Stays Dome, he knew he was subject to the rules just like everyone else.

And one of those rules—the one about *not* trespassing in the Lunar Caverns—had been broken.

Since he saw no point of *pretending* to peruse his microscope when Mackenzie entered, he straightened up and—holding his hands clasped down at his waist—waited patiently. She wouldn't get any sort of a rise out of him; of that he was certain.

He refused to expend any energy on anger.

He would be practical.

He would do what he could to bargain for Louise's continuing service within the Celestial Stays Dome. He would claim—*rightly*—that it'd all been his own idea. And that Louise hadn't fully understood the implications of what she had agreed to do.

When someone did come through the doorway, though, it wasn't who he expected.

It wasn't Mackenzie.

He was taken aback not to see the flamey redhead at all.

Instead, it was silver-haired Wendy . . . the one who had caught him, and Louise, in the Caverns the night before. And she didn't even wear so much as a frown.

In fact, unless Njhay was very, very mistaken, she was *smiling*.

"Morning," she said.

"Morning," Njhay just about managed to mutter by way of reply.

She took a few steps into the lab, approaching her own desk, as if this was just another ordinary day at work. "Turned up anything interesting overnight?"

Njhay was stunned for a couple of seconds, and then his brain nudged him, informed him that she was really saying what he believed —that she was merely asking about his work. "Oh," he replied, turning around, shifting a glance off at his microscope, as if the device itself was going to give him an answer. "No, nothing, uh, *unusual.*"

Wendy arrived at her desk and considered something.

She drifted into silence.

A great sense of unease descended upon the room . . . or at least it did over Njhay.

As if everything was normal, he returned to his microscope, trying to implement the façade of him going to work as usual. Perhaps this wouldn't be as big of a deal as he'd made it out to be.

Finally, after about ten minutes had passed, and with the two of them apparently busy with their own particular jobs, Njhay glanced back at Wendy, who glanced back at him. The two of them stared one another down for the longest time before a smile gripped the corners of Wendy's mouth.

Against all odds, Njhay found himself smiling back.

"I don't have to tell you to take care," she said, her smile slackening a touch.

Feeling his chest tighten, a slight tingle pass up his spine, he replied, "No."

"Good," Wendy said, turning back to her work. "Because she's a sensitive girl—*vulnerable.*" She stopped speaking and the room drifted into silence. Then she said, "Easily *damaged.*"

Njhay stood staring at the back of Wendy's overalls for a few moments before something snapped at the back of his brain and he returned to his work.

As he peered down through the eyepiece of his microscope, he couldn't help but feel the smile breaking out at the corners of his mouth.

It was like being a naughty schoolchild.

25

BREAKFAST INITIATED

at in the breakfast room of the Lunar Grand, Alex stared at the waitress pouring the freshly squeezed orange juice into his glass. He watched as the bright liquid squirted up against the glass.

He breathed in the zesty scent of it.

He could feel that parched longing on his tongue . . . the need to *taste* that rich, sugary nectar.

That need to *focus* on something; to channel his *rage* onto something.

"*Buenos Días.*"

Alex glanced up. He hardly had time to check himself—to press on his professional, business-like smile. He met Costantino Zito's eye. "Good morning," Alex replied, deciding against testing out his less-than-rudimentary Spanish.

He noted that Gofreddo—Costantino's son—was present too.

He greeted him, offered him a place at the empty table.

The waitress retreated, the orange juice having been poured.

Alex straightened up in his chair, peering over the glass of juice as Costantino and Gofreddo took their places.

"What's the plan today, then?" Alex said, doing his best to smile from ear to ear.

He knew, from all the books he'd studied—from all those *social skills* courses he'd taken—that the simple act of smiling would get him very far indeed. It didn't really matter whether or not he meant it deep down. Humans were surface creatures; oblivious to the details . . . even a man like Costantino—he supposed—was oblivious to his *exact* thoughts.

Sure enough, Costantino mirrored Alex's smile.

None the wiser.

"I was just telling Fred about last night," Costantino said. "About that *very interesting* sighting we had on our way out of the Caverns."

"Oh," Alex said, unable to stop himself from flushing but somehow managing to keep up his smile. "Yes."

He couldn't believe there was anything *more* humiliating than what had befallen him the night before. Not only to have happened upon an ex-lover—on the *Moon* no less—but to find her in a state of *sordid* circumstances . . . and looking so *happy* . . . *glowing* almost.

What was more, Fiona had refused to so much as go around with him today. She had complained of a headache and claimed that she wanted to stay in bed all day. And then they'd fought. He had put it to her that she would—*most likely*—never again have the opportunity to travel to the Moon; and she had put it to him that she couldn't care less.

It had been an uncouth scene.

And one which had left Alex in a *foul* mood.

Which made maintaining the smile all the more difficult.

"What's for breakfast?" Costantino asked.

"Huh?" Alex replied, bluntly, unable to catch himself in time.

He realised that his smile had slipped, too.

He saw to that.

Took a deep breath.

And thought of the potential *profit*.

"I'm having poached eggs," Alex replied, meeting Costantino's now-uneasy expression.

It was just as he had heard; all those stories of how Costantino was a unreasonably *perceptive* individual—often calling off some business deal or other because of some minor detail: how a potential business partner had treated a waiter, or other functionary; because of poor personal hygiene; or, perhaps the most famous rumour of them all, how he had once cancelled a deal at the eleventh hour because someone had thought it funny to insult a junior member of the company.

Alex had been so careful to avoid any of *these* pitfalls. Although things were made somewhat easier given that the pair of them were on holiday. The atmosphere was more relaxed.

This made it—as any predator worth its salt knew—the *perfect* time to strike.

As Costantino and Gofreddo consulted their menus, Alex searched for something to say. He glanced over Gofreddo's face, saw the pair of dark bags hanging down from his eye sockets; decided *that* wouldn't be a particularly astute observation to make . . . from what Alex had gathered down through the years, men were inordinately proud of their sons.

While Alex thought hard on what he wanted to say, he couldn't help but cast his mind back to Louise. How she'd looked last night.

Flustered . . . caught in the act?

. . . Louise *Williams* . . .

In a way he couldn't quite imagine *how* he had let her go.

He had been good to her; had helped her get on in the company . . . and then, one day, she'd mysteriously disappeared . . . simply gone *AWOL* . . .

It perplexed Alex, even now.

The waitress returned to take both Costantino and Gofreddo's orders, and then, as quickly as she'd come, she retreated.

Alex was conscious of—all the time—aiming a bright and perky smile at the waitress in case Costantino should scrutinise him.

Once the waitress had gone, he looked back to Costantino and Gofreddo.

"Do you happen to know who'll be *looking after* us today?"

Costantino smiled back at him warmly. "From what I've heard we have the pleasure of the company of the young lady from the night before, Louise Williams." His smile seemed to widen further still. "I had a word with the superiors of the Dome, making sure that neither she nor her companion would get into trouble; it is the last thing I would want for somebody to get into trouble because of me."

Alex gritted his teeth and smiled back. "Of course," he replied, at the same time thinking that—if something similar had occurred at Humble Associates—he would've been sure to put the entire matter about town; to warn other potential employers about these *unrefined* elements of the workforce.

"A wonderful young woman," Costantino said, mostly to himself. "So kind and thoughtful."

Alex turned his attention back to his orange juice.

Stared into its bright colour.

And then said, "Yes, yes she is," in a quiet voice only he could hear.

26

BUSINESS AS USUAL

*L*ouise had hardly slept at all during the night.

The two of them—*her and Njhay*—getting caught in the Lunar Caverns had left her expecting an entire cohort of Security to come bursting in through her door in the middle of the night.

She could've sworn that—*by now*—sitting in a PEAR, headed for the Lunar Grand, she would've been on a Shuttle headed back to Earth.

The only explanation she could come up with was that Celestial Stays couldn't bear to lose face with Costantino. From the stories she'd heard, his employee management was nearly the stuff of legend. In one story she'd heard—and she wasn't convinced as to its veracity—Costantino had taken into his home not only an employee but his *entire family* when their own house had flooded.

How anybody could have been painted as such a good-hearted individual, Louise knew had to be the result of a comprehensive spin doctor, or else because the person was genuinely, well . . . *good*.

She left the PEAR behind, hoiking herself up and over the side, and then she set off to greet her guests. They were already waiting for her in the hotel lobby.

Right away, she couldn't help but notice how they'd lost another one . . . that only Costantino and Alex were here today. Her heart clenched. And her blood ran hot. Her eyes skirted over Alex's, and she shifted her attention onto Costantino . . . her mind wheeled back to the instructions which Mackenzie had given her; that she was supposed to *spy* on the man.

And just *what* she was supposed to report remained something of a mystery.

She smiled—not a difficult thing to do when Costantino was doing it all the time. "Seems as if you're dropping like flies."

"Yes," Costantino replied, throwing his hand up, and pulling a mock grimace. "My son—he said that he does not *feel* so well."

And then—because she felt she had to—she turned to Alex, and said, "What about your *fiancée*? Isn't she coming along for the trip?"

"No," Alex replied, flatly, concisely, and then, shifting a sidelong glance at Costantino, added, "She's got a *headache*."

"I'm sorry to hear it," Louise replied, and then, considering her training—what *training* she'd hurriedly been given by Mackenzie— she said, "Would you like a doctor?"

Alex merely shook his head and mumbled, "No, thank you."

Since Louise had very little help from the itinerary for that day —it merely read 'free time'—she decided to take them along to the Crescent Gardens; it being the part of the Dome which she knew best by far.

Even as they left the PEAR behind, Louise couldn't help

wondering whether this might be something of a comedown, considering that, the last time the two of them had been in the Gardens, there had been all sorts of glowing, sparkling magic going on.

However, if Costantino was anything but delighted, he didn't show it.

Throughout the impromptu tour, helped on its way when Wendy arrived, Costantino asked—what sounded to Louise— intelligent questions.

Alex lagged near the back of the procession.

Several times, Louise found the two of them walking side by side. She did her best to rectify this by either speeding up or slowing down her pace . . . on one occasion, when it seemed that Alex had cottoned onto her evasive tactics, she'd dropped down and feigned to tie her shoelace.

When they reached the end of the Gardens, they decided it would be a good idea to take some lunch. As if by magic, a member of the Hospitality staff appeared out of thin air with a picnic hamper. They settled down, with Wendy mercifully tagging along, on one of the patches of grass.

Even now, even more than a week after having set down on the Moon, Louise couldn't help but find it incredible to simply glance upward and see the Earth dominating her vision.

Every time it drew her attention, she remained fixated . . . for so long she was sure—if she didn't draw herself back—she might lose her mind.

She had heard all those stories which dealt with space dementia, and she knew that it continued to be a large and constantly growing area of study. And she wasn't all that keen to find herself included among the test subjects.

It was during the picnic, while Costantino was chomping the

bit with Wendy over some botany-related matter or other that Alex turned into Louise and spoke.

She was taken aback by how steadily he gazed at her.

His eyes widening.

Taking her in as she could never remember him doing so before.

If this alone startled her, then she was all the more surprised to feel his hand clasp over her own.

"You know," he said, the level of his voice dropped down, so that they wouldn't be overheard by either Wendy or Costantino, "I never heard anything more from you after that day; you simply just up and disappeared." He made a *poof* gesture with his hands. "Never so much as another word. When I came home—to the flat —everything was gone."

Louise shifted a glance in Wendy and Costantino's direction, but they continued to be wrapped up in whatever conversation it was they were having. She turned her attention back onto Alex, knowing that she needed to remain professional. That she needed to remain *balanced* . . .

"I had to leave," Louise replied, impressed at how she struck a flat tone of voice.

Her eyes focussed in on his.

She was certain she saw something lurking there, toward the backs of his eyes . . . what it was, though, she couldn't say. Or perhaps it frightened her to say.

His hand was a little sweaty, and it pinned her own down to the grass. She wanted—more than anything—to tell him to let go . . . to tell him to *leave her alone.*

But she couldn't make a scene; not when any little thing might spoil everything for her employer.

For Celestial Stays.

First and foremost, she had made a commitment to them.

"We could make a great team," Alex said, apparently ignoring her last comment. "I'm *convinced* of that . . . we *were* a great team until you decided to leave."

As Alex stared into her eyes, she knew, quite simply, that she couldn't take another moment of it. Working quickly, and—she hoped—subtly, she writhed her hand out from beneath Alex's.

Although she knew, if he wished, he had the strength to overcome her, he didn't try . . . he was surely being watched just as closely by Costantino and, as such, was just as worried about slipping up in some way.

Her hand away from Alex's and feeling like she had a little room to breathe, she got up to her feet, and then, with a bright smile aimed at Wendy, said, "Could we have a quick chat—*alone?*"

Fortunately, Wendy and Costantino had broken off their conversation a couple of moments sooner, so there was no need for Louise to interrupt them . . . she would've been loath to do so.

Wendy shot Costantino an apologetic glance, then got up to her feet. "We'll be back in a minute," she said, brushing some crumbs from her sandwich off the front of her overalls. "If you absolutely *have* to go raiding those blueberry muffins then at the very least leave one for me . . . I'd hate to have to call up Alicia and get her to bake some more."

Costantino chuckled, and, Louise couldn't help noticing him reaching for the picnic hamper; apparently where the blueberry muffins were located.

As they walked away from the two men, Louise couldn't help but notice the sly smile which clung to Wendy's lips. "What?" she said, her interest piqued.

" 'What' yourself," Wendy replied, but that smile never let up.

"Seems like you've been getting close to our distinguished guest."

"Oh," Wendy said, batting her hand. "It's just *business*."

Louise glanced over her shoulder, seeing that Costantino was studying them closely. That his eyes were fixed on both of them . . . or, at least, *one* of them.

When she turned back to Wendy, she saw that she was blushing. "You *minx*."

"*What?*"

"You're leading him *on*."

"I'm doing nothing of the sort."

Louise eyed her closely, unsure of this claim.

Wendy shook her head, then held up her palm as if to dismiss the matter once and for all. "Okay," she said. "What was so urgent that it necessitated me withdrawing my apparently python-like hold on Señor Zito?"

Louise glanced back to the pair of them; to Costantino and Alex . . . it was like something out of a bad dream—yeah, like her *worst* nightmare . . .

"It's getting weird," Louise said. "I mean, the stuff he's been saying . . . he's being *nice* to me."

Wendy regarded Louise. She held her stare. " 'Weird' how?"

"He, I don't know, held my hand."

"He *held* your hand?"

Wendy's voice sounded as outraged as Louise felt about the whole deal.

Louise watched on as Wendy's complexion darkened; the fury setting in.

She narrowed her eyes then thrust her finger into Louise's chest. "You're going to the lab—*right now*—and then you're going to return to the Basements; where you're to await further instructions."

"Whoa, whoa, whoa!" Louise said, unable to help herself—feeling as if she was making mountains out of molehills now. She had only wanted a timeout . . . to share how *weird* this whole situation had become. "It'll be fine," she continued, "I promise . . . I just . . ."

But she caught herself looking over at Costantino and Alex all over again. She couldn't help the old feelings coming back to her: the anger, the *obsession* . . . the feeling that she would *never* be the only one for Alex; that he would *always* be striving for another.

He could never *be* content with just one.

Not like her.

"Listen," Wendy continued, "your mind is all screwed up, okay? You need to have some space of your own. Let me take care of all this, then you can, you know, see how you feel about it later on."

As if this decided everything, Wendy turned back toward the two men having the picnic.

Louise remained standing where she was for another few moments, unsure quite what to do.

In the end, catching Alex's eye was the catalyst—the spark which moved her off the spot.

As Wendy had instructed her, she headed quickly toward the lab.

Just as she was about to slip out of sight of the picnic, she couldn't resist one glance back. She caught Alex's eye. She saw the anger there—*hurt*—but, most of all, she saw an unquenchable *desire* . . .

179

INTERRUPTION

*A*s *Njhay worked away* at his microscope, he had managed to slip away to another world; to that portion of his mind which was fully focussed on his work. Sometimes he wondered if other people could carry off the same trick that he could; if they could simply put on blinders and leave everything else behind.

He wondered if it was this frame of mind which led to the discovery of emaciated bodies—several months later—dead of thirst or starvation because there was nobody around to call them away from their *important* work.

Well, if that was how it was to end, Njhay couldn't say that he'd be disappointed.

His life, after all, *was* his work . . . or it had been until—

Outside, in the corridor, he could hear the pounding of footsteps. He turned just in time to see Louise bounding toward him. Before he could react in any way—even before he could so much as smile—she leaped at him, throwing her arms about his neck.

Njhay somehow managed to steady himself up against the lab counter.

Luckily, he missed his microscope.

It was a pleasant surprise—but a *surprise* nonetheless—and he hadn't even had a chance to relocate his glasses to a safe spot before he'd been jumped. His glasses spun free of the place where they had rested on his scalp, flew through the air and landed on the floor with a plastic rattle.

He caught a quick glance of where they landed, working more with a sense of survival than anything else . . . without his glasses it was a real hassle to get about.

He breathed in Louise; her lemony, just-showered scent.

Before he could really concentrate on anything, Louise pressed her lips up against his.

He had little choice but to kiss her back.

Her tongue pushed forth into his mouth with great hunger.

He gave as good as he got.

Finally able to free himself of her mouth—to somehow sate her thirst—he got out some words. "What . . ." he said, realising that he was panting for breath ". . . *What's* this all about?"

Louise arched an eyebrow, smirked. "Not pleased to see me?"

"Yes, I mean . . . *no*, I am . . . it's just I wasn't expecting that . . ."

He trailed off unwittingly.

Louise picked up his slack. "It's just that you weren't *expecting* something to interrupt your work?"

Njhay smiled. "Something like that."

He glanced to the floor, where he sensed his glasses had dropped.

He tried to move past her.

She blocked his path.

"Just where do you *think* you're going?" she said.

"I . . . uh . . ." His eyes returned to hers, and he realised he was lost.

Completely and utterly.

Hopelessly.

Lost.

As she pushed him onto his back, and he felt the steady, unstoppable heat rising through his body, he listened to what she told him.

"I want to hear something," she said. "I want to hear you *say* something."

"What?" he replied, feeling himself being eased down onto the metal examination table. "What do you want to hear?"

Louise held him down firmly, apparently decided to keep him in his spot. "I want to hear that you'll stay with me—that you'll stay up here, on the *Moon*, with me . . ."

Njhay's mind felt as if it might burst. He couldn't quite wrestle his eyes off hers. And, at the same time, he felt her well-toned, shapely body up against his.

He knew he wouldn't be able to bear it much longer.

"Louise," he said, his voice escaping almost as a gasp. "I think you might be the most beautiful, most perfect woman I've ever met." He paused a beat, widened his eyes. "Will that do?"

But, before she took the time to reply, her mouth was already pressed—*hungrily*—to his own.

And he submitted.

2 8

COMMITMENT

ater that day, back in her room in the Basements, Louise spun through the messages left to her on the Link.

Although there was one from Mackenzie, she decided to defer it for the time being.

Already it felt as if she'd spent too much time delving into the past today . . . she had spent too much of her mental energy on *Alex Barn*.

Her attention was instantly drawn to a message from Njhay.

She opened it and prepared herself.

Because she couldn't quite believe that anything this good—anything that felt *this right*—could go off without a hitch . . . she had been just waiting for the message outlining his cold feet to come through; it would be a relief to get it over and done with. The Link read the message to her in its cool, gender-neutral voice:

Louise,

I remember a time when I was younger, when it was customary for young lovers to send one another paper romantic notes. But since we have no paper here, on the Moon, I suppose that this note through the Link will just have to do.

The past week or so in which we've become acquainted has been one of the happiest, most incredible, *weeks of my life. And I just wanted to write this note to you to assure you that I keep you in mind always—even when I appear to be most steeped in my work.*

Nothing else matters to me. I want to be with you.

I love you,

Njhay

As Louise heard the message reverberate within her skull, a prickling sensation passed across the surface of her skin. Her brain couldn't quite make the connection. She couldn't *quite* believe that this was real . . . that he had actually come out and *said it*.

In all her past relationships, it had always fallen to her to be the one to say it first; the one who needed to declare her *love* first.

What did it *mean*?

Was he different from the others?

She at least knew enough to say that he was different from Alex Barn . . .

With a gentle inhalation, Louise turned her mind to the other messages awaiting her. The one from Mackenzie. As usual, even though it wasn't Mackenzie's voice at all, Louise could sense the urgency sparking free of the words.

She wanted to meet right away.

Louise knew there could only be one explanation; that, in cahoots with Wendy, Mackenzie had decided on a plan-of-action concerning Alex Barn.

On her way out of her room, Louise nearly bumped right into Kyra Singh.

With a flash of her eyes—*a slight smile*—Kyra apologised and then sauntered off along the hall; apparently headed back to her own room.

It was strange to think how often Louise ended up bumping into Kyra. She always seemed to be delving into some corner of the Dome . . . *exploring* something.

During the visit to the Apollo 11 landing site, Kyra had revealed that, in her life down on Earth, she'd been a journalist, and that all these tours she was now having to get herself involved in were 'below' what she believed to be her real talents.

Once Louise had left her behind, she ventured up in the lift. She happened to catch it with Alicia Brennan, who, when Louise asked her where she was headed, turned as red as one of those radishes Njhay had managed to make grow in the Crescent Gardens.

Alicia was still blushing when she waved Louise goodbye and stepped into her PEAR . . . apparently heading off to the Orbital Café to go and catch up with her business.

According to the message, Louise was to meet with Mackenzie in her office; located on one of the top floors of the Lunar Grand.

It felt strange to be in the lobby of the Lunar Grand and not to be there to meet with Costantino Zito. She felt a strange sense of sadness at the fact, as if Costantino had taken on some sort of a role as an honorary grandfather in her mind.

Mackenzie's floor in the Lunar Grand was filled with glass windows, peering down over the Celestial Stays Dome. Soon enough, she noted the augmented programming within the windows which would allow the viewer to zoom in on any detail taking place below.

Louise decided this had to be the brain centre.

Where Mackenzie kept her finger on the pulse.

Mackenzie's office walls consisted of glass and Louise could see her striding back and forth at the other end of her office, finger thrust deeply into her inner-ear; sending some order or other.

Louise wondered if she should knock, but, seeing the door was already open, she decided against it. She simply trod into the office, and waited for Mackenzie to turn around.

When she did, she held up a commanding finger to Louise, as if to say that she would just be a minute with this order. She finished up whatever it was she was sorting out within the Celestial Stays Dome and then smiled broadly. She indicated the chairs—*both glass* —which stood before her desk . . . *also* made of glass.

Louise did as she was told, taking a seat opposite Mackenzie, while Mackenzie herself only perched on the edge of her desk; those alarmingly bright-green eyes of hers trapping Louise well and truly.

"So," Mackenzie said, "Wendy told me the whole deal." She twitched her nose. "Why didn't you say anything sooner?"

Louise *had* explained to Wendy. And they had decided she could cope.

That this could be Louise's greatest victory.

. . . But then Alex had begun to act . . . *strangely.*

Mackenzie tilted her head to one side, narrowed one eyelid to a slit, and then said, "And how've you been holding up—with *them?*"

"With who?" Louise replied, feeling a little ditsy for a moment —forgetting what it was they were talking about. "Oh," she put in, snapping back to reality. "Well, I suppose I've been getting used to it"—Louise couldn't help but notice Mackenzie eyeing her closely —"I mean, there've been a few uncomfortable moments, but, apart from that, it's been fine." She put on a smile. "*Really.*"

Mackenzie continued to stare her down. Louise held still.

Tried to stay *strong.*

But that was easier said than done as she felt a tear escaping the corner of her eye, and rolling down her cheek.

As if this was some sort of victory, Mackenzie gave a slight smile. Then she reached out for Louise, resting her hand on her shoulder. She squeezed tightly.

Louise supposed this was the closest Mackenzie ever got to actually *hugging* anybody.

"Listen," Mackenzie said, "I am so proud of you—and, what's more, from all of the information I've relayed to her, I can tell you that Karolin Köhler is extremely impressed." She tapped the side of her nose. "From all the signals—all the *ears to the ground*—it seems that Costantino Zito is *delighted* about the attention he's received this far."

Despite everything, despite the chilly tear track lining her cheek, she felt a warmth spark to life within her chest. It felt nice to be told that she'd done well; that she'd done a 'good job'. And yet there was fear, too; a lingering worry that she might be getting into deeper waters; that she might well be finding herself in a trickier position than she had so far.

"How do you feel," Mackenzie continued, "about playing hostess for another few days? How do you feel about looking after them—continuing the great work you've already begun?"

Louise felt a tightness across her gut. It lingered there for a long moment, and then, finally, as if she'd merely had to exhale to ease herself of the unpleasant sensation, it was gone.

And she felt a fresh new confidence rising through her.

She stared back into Mackenzie's laser-green eyes.

"Okay," she replied, firmly and decidedly.

Mackenzie smiled back at her. "Good," she said, slipping off the edge of her desk, and returning to her two feet. "Then let's get you hopping to it, shall we?"

29

ULTIMATUM

It was a rare occasion when Njhay felt incapable of stopping himself from whistling, but now was one of those times. He felt the shrill—*surely tone-deaf*—notes rattle out through his pursed lips.

As he crossed the lab, flipped his glasses up onto the top of his head, he noticed that there was a skip to his step . . . almost like he was dancing.

All of a sudden feeling somewhat self-conscious, he glanced about himself, sure that somebody might be watching. There was nobody, though, of course. Not in the Crescent Gardens lab. This was the place even the most curious of lunar tourists tended to give a wide berth.

Content that he was alone now, and unable to quite keep the pleasant hum in his chest to himself, he took up his whistling as he peered down through the eyepiece of the microscope. It was only after what could've been ten minutes—or as long as an hour—that he heard those smart, no-nonsense footsteps.

He would've known them anywhere, but he most certainly recognised them here.

Although he considered the lab something of a hiding place, he couldn't help but admit to himself that it was a hiding place which just about *everybody* knew of . . . perhaps he should think up a new location.

He backed away from his microscope, straightened himself up and replaced his glasses over the bridge of his nose. He knew that it was usually of benefit to be able to see during these sorts of encounters.

Sure enough, Supervisor Mackenzie Angliss strode on in through the doorway. As was par for the course, she wore a thunderous expression which belay the—*surely*—many hundreds of things she'd rather be doing than interfacing with him. Her red hair was tied into a tight bun around the back of her head and her whip-smart green eyes immediately locked him in her gaze.

"García? We've got to talk."

Since the successful display Njhay had put on for Costantino Zito—not to mention the personal dinner he'd been invited to afterward—he had been feeling somewhat more confident about things. About his position within the Celestial Stays Dome . . . that unpleasant situation of getting caught in the Lunar Caverns by Wendy apart, of course . . .

This time, he found the strength to stand up straight—to *not* allow Angliss to tramp all over him, as she so often did. "Do we?" he replied.

Angliss pursed her lips and frown lines appeared in her forehead. He knew that this certainly wasn't the way to get on her good side. However, she made no mention to this half-hearted suggestion of rebellion. "I've heard rumours," she said.

" 'Rumours' ?" Njhay replied, flashing his eyebrows, surprising himself when he felt a shred of anger pass through his gut. "And what *rumours* would those be?"

"Rumours concerning you and Louise Williams."

Njhay's heart leaped in his chest.

He felt a chill pass through his blood.

His mind seemed to ebb wide, expanding—*returning*—to the night before . . . it was hard to believe that a woman could make him feel like this again; as if nothing at all had ever happened.

Almost as if his heart had never even been broken.

Almost.

"Look," Angliss said, holding up her palm, and, after jabbing her finger into her earpiece—sending an order to God-knew-who—she went on, "I don't need to know the details, but you and I know the Dome rumour mill better than anyone . . . I'm not going to bore you with clichés about 'smoke and fire'; I just want an assurance from you."

It was Njhay's turn to frown. "What assurance?"

Again acting casually, Angliss jabbed her finger into her earpiece, sending off yet another order. "I want you to break it off."

It felt as if he'd been punched in the gut. "Excuse me?"

Angliss nodded in reply. "You heard me."

Njhay was rendered stunned for several seconds.

In the time it took him to regain his senses, Angliss had already turned around and was heading out of the door. Acting before thinking, he leaped the few steps over to her and grabbed hold of the sleeve of her overalls. When Angliss turned to face him, he was nearly convinced that she was going to strike him. Instead, though, she muttered, matter-of-factly—*professionally*—without any hint of emotion, "I'll have Security here within the minute."

Njhay squeezed tighter, and then—realising what he was doing—he released her.

Angliss smoothed out the wrinkles in her overalls. Seeing that Njhay had backed off several steps, she brought her hand down from her ear, where it had been hovering, apparently ready to call in Security at a second's notice. "Listen to me, García," Angliss went on. "Louise is potentially very valuable to Celestial Stays; she's proven her worth in how she's dealt with Costantino Zito. We'd like to do everything in our power to keep her here. *Karolin Köhler* would like to do everything in her power to keep her *here*. The last thing we want is for her to become upset and decide to leave." Angliss blew out a long sigh. "You've gotten to know her in the time she's been here; you know how vulnerable she is . . ."

Here Angliss trailed off.

Njhay shook his head. "Sorry," he said. "I don't think I'm quite following you."

Angliss met his eye. "Come on, I'm sure she's told you all about her past life—about what actually *drove* her up to the Moon?"

Njhay held himself very still.

His heart hung in his throat.

Again, he shook his head.

"Well," Angliss replied, her smile firm, unmoving, "then it's not my place to tell you . . . you'd be better off hearing it from her."

Njhay stared back at Angliss.

Any anger he'd been feeling was gone now.

Replaced by a sense of understanding.

"Those people—the couple accompanying Costantino . . . do they have anything to do with Louise?"

"Listen to me, Njhay, and listen to me *carefully*."

His attention drifted away from his wonderings and he channelled his full focus onto Angliss.

It wasn't often—if *ever*—that she used his first name.

And now that she had, he wasn't sure he liked it.

Angliss continued, "You've carried out an awful lot of useful research here—during your time at Celestial Stays—and, far be it from me to draw any conclusions on your future plans; on whether or not you decide to continue your service . . ."

Njhay could feel a big 'but' coming.

"*But,*" Angliss went on, "if the rumours of you wishing to leave Celestial Stays behind following the completion of your current rotation *are* true then it is in your best interest for Celestial Stays to sign off on the work you've done here. So that you can continue to explore these—no doubt *fascinating*—areas of research Earthside."

Njhay's gut tightened.

He felt a searing heat in his chest.

He concentrated all his energy on maintaining a neutral expression.

He couldn't *show* any emotion.

"How many rotations have you completed with Celestial Stays, García?"

"Three," he replied, deadpan.

Angliss whistled flat and shrill; an eardrum-piercing sound. "My," she continued, "you really *must* have a great deal of material."

"About a decade's worth."

Angliss pressed on a smirk. "And it would be such a shame to throw that all away; just because you couldn't let this girl go." She took a step toward him, placed her hand on his shoulder. "Believe me, there will be others, Njhay—don't throw your life's work away just because you *fell in love.*"

Angliss's grip felt like acid to his skin.

But he didn't shrug her off.

He *couldn't* shrug her off.

Finally, she released him, and padded away.

A sudden flood of rage pumped through his blood. He clenched his fists down at his sides; ready to do what he needed to so that he might escape this blackmail attempt.

Angliss had surely never been in love herself; if she *had been* then she would be able to see what a *huge* deal this was.

Angliss lingered in the doorway, turning to speak parting words to him over her shoulder. "If you accept the terms, then I can have you on Costantino's Shuttle back, in a couple of days. From a personal perspective, I don't see the point in delaying something once you've made up your mind . . . what difference would it make to wait out the completion of your rotation if you've already set your heart on returning to Earth?"

He wondered if she would flash a grin at him—*some sort of victory smirk*—but she retained her cold, professional exterior. And Njhay was left only with the sound of her departing footsteps off down the corridor.

Once the footsteps had completely quietened, he reached up for his glasses, resting on his scalp. He tugged them free from where they'd become snarled in his curly hair and he tossed them away—*across the lab.*

They landed with a pair of plasticky *thunks.*

And then there was only silence.

The gentle, percussive, *thump-thump* of his heart.

30

AWOL

*W*hen *Louise* returned to the Basements, she received her new brief from Mackenzie; the plan-of-action for Costantino over the coming days.

She flipped through the details, finally coming across the warm assurance—well, it *was* 'warm' coming from Mackenzie—wishing her 'Good Luck'.

As Louise had thought things over on the way back in the PEAR, she had become stuck on the idea that what she'd done— that what she'd *achieved*—over the past days had surely been what she'd always strived for . . . hadn't she always *wanted* to be acknowledged for her own best efforts?

Hadn't she *always* wanted to go it alone?

. . . Make it without some 'sugar daddy' looming in the background . . .

With her mind partially fixed on the next instalment of the entertainment programme, she worked to prod an earring through her earlobe; jabbing her tongue out as she did so. She thought about how Alex had frequently commented on this habit of hers, when she would—*quite unconsciously*—thrust her tongue out of the corner of her mouth. He had often told her that it was 'unbecoming' and even 'embarrassing'; especially when she did it in meetings, apparently . . .

Well, Alex wasn't here, in her bedroom, to tell her any different now.

Louise had barely zipped up her overalls—getting ready to shoot off and meet with Costantino and the rest of the group—when the Link informed her that there was somebody at her door.

Of course, she allowed them in . . . a mite surprised to note that it was a woman called Lan Niu.

. . . It took Louise another few seconds to recall that she'd met her before—if *met* was the right word to use . . .

Sure enough, when Louise ordered the door to slide open, she took in the black overalls of the Security personnel. And how her plaited, black hair seemed to be thick and strong enough to garrotte some unsuspecting individual.

Confused for a moment, Louise frowned, then said, "What is it? What's the matter?"

Lin remained straight-faced, her eyes meeting Louise's.

All business.

Sometimes Louise wondered if the simple act of putting on a uniform affected a person's personality.

"One of your guests," Niu replied. "Gone missing."

Louise felt as if someone had knocked her back several steps.

"I'm sorry," she said, "I don't . . . what does this *mean*?"

Niu glanced beyond Louise, into her room, as if she might be harbouring whoever it was who had gone missing. There was, of course, nobody but her in the room.

Niu returned to Louise. "One of the Security briefs is to keep a careful eye on all of our guests; to ensure that they don't endanger themselves or others . . . one of these policies involves knowing the basic whereabouts of every person."

Louise stared back into Niu's eyes, still unable to comprehend.

Finally, she got out the question she most wanted answered.

"Who was it? Who's gone missing?"

Niu pursed her lips, cocked her head to one side. "Alex Barn," she said, stating his name evenly, matter-of-factly.

And it sent a chill through Louise's gut.

Louise was standing in the hallway, outside Alex and Fiona's suite, before she quite got her head around what had befallen her. She glanced to Niu, seeing that she held her hand over the grip of her holstered blaster pistol at her thigh.

Niu nodded to Louise, and Louise requested entrance to the suite.

She received an answer near-instantly.

The doors swept back to reveal the expansive room beyond.

It was all set in darkness. Louise quickly took itinerary of the drapes hanging down; the windows which looked out across the Dome all covered up . . . she wondered—if she had come up to the Moon, as a guest—if she would've *ever* thought to block out the scenery.

Then again, she did suppose there was a matter of privacy to consider.

Louise moved past the lush carpets, and over to the enormous four-poster bed, which, despite its size, didn't dominate the room by any means.

Lying on top, with her back to them, Louise made out Fiona.

With a quick glance back to Niu, and a gentle nod that she could proceed, Louise approached the bed. She took care, not because she was afraid that Fiona might be armed, or that she might be dangerous in some way . . . no, it was more of a reverence for the emotional turmoil which Louise had sensed hanging in the air.

As she knew from personal experience, whenever someone was attempting to get information from someone *else* it was generally conducive to keep that person in a balanced state of mind.

Louise rounded the bed and crouched down before Fiona.

She had her eyes shut, her knees tucked up to her chest, almost in a foetal position. When Louise closed the gap between their faces, she could hear her humming some unidentifiable tune in a low voice, at the back of her throat.

"Fiona?" Louise said, making an effort to keep her voice soft and smooth. "It's me, *Louise.*"

Fiona remained still.

She was taking deep breaths, absorbing them right down to the pit of her stomach.

When she retreated slightly, Louise noted the bruise on her cheek.

A pang passed through her gut.

It felt as if she was sinking; as if she had only to not concentrate for a moment and the ground would swallow her up. She pushed the feeling away, tried her best to stay focussed. She had a task now; to see to Fiona . . . to locate *Alex.*

Slowly, Fiona fluttered an eyelid open.

Her eyes were slightly damp, as if she was still coming around from sleep.

Louise glanced up, saw that Niu was keeping an eye on the

doorway, clearly concerned about Alex Barn coming rushing through at any moment.

Taking pains to be as tender as she could manage, Louise reached out and laid her hand over Fiona's. She felt her tremble slightly at her touch. "Fiona?" Louise repeated. "We're looking for Alex—we need to know where Alex has got to . . . do you think you can tell us?"

Fiona lay still, made no response.

Louise glanced back, and then over to Niu. She felt slightly more confident, though she wasn't sure exactly *why*. "Get the curtains, will you? Let some light into the room."

As if Louise was her superior, Niu snapped into action, marching over to the curtains and then drawing them open in even, efficient sweeps.

Now that the bedroom was set in a better light, Louise could see, for the first time, what sort of a state it was in. How the whole place had—for want of a better term—been totally trashed.

Apparently also having taken stock of the room, Niu reached up for her earpiece. When Louise met her eye, she explained, "I need to call this in now." She gave something between a sneer and a wry smile. "We've got certain protocols we need to adhere to."

Louise turned her attention back onto Fiona, who was blinking herself around from her daze. She sniffed several times, sucking in air, getting her breath back.

That was good.

Louise knew, from experience, that, if the state of the room was anything to go by, Fiona would need some time to recover from the fight which'd occurred previously.

She helped Fiona up into a sitting position, with her back resting against the headboard.

Fiona's eyes seemed to lose focus, and then—*with a rapid series of blinks*—to return to reality after a long delay. "Gone," she said, her voice so quiet, so *weak* as to be rendered nearly inaudible.

"Yes," Louise replied, nodding, "but *where* . . . where has he gone *to*?"

All of a sudden, Fiona locked eyes with her. Her lips parted slightly. And then she let out a low, almost uncanny *moan*. ". . . Sorry . . . I'm so *sorry* . . ."

Louise stared back into her eyes, unable to quite fathom what it was Fiona was sorry for.

Finally, Fiona reached up her hand and indicated Louise's temple; and the bruise there.

"It's okay," Louise replied. "Really, don't worry about it . . . water under the bridge, and all that."

Despite this assurance, Fiona's expression didn't shift.

Outside the suite, Louise could hear footsteps—people coming along the hallway.

She turned and looked to the door, saw that Niu was half in the suite and half out in the corridor.

"What's happening?" Louise just about got out. "What's *going on*?"

Niu glanced back at Louise, smiled slightly. "Protocol," she replied.

Louise turned back to Fiona, seeing that she had closed her eyes once again; that she was retreating into the safe place she had constructed to deal with Alex's temper tantrums. As Louise's eyes left Fiona's behind, she found her attention being drawn to the bedside table.

On top, she caught sight of a takeaway package from the Orbital Café . . . the package had been opened and the contents thoroughly devoured; all that remained of the interior were the greasy spots where the pastries had been laid out lovingly by Alicia.

Her attention drifted down.

To the open door of the bedside cabinet.

She spotted, as clearly as daylight, the case within.

The foam inner lining.

Forming the shape of what was—*without doubt*—a blaster pistol.

Hearing someone calling her from the room—telling her that she had to go while the professionals took over—she batted the door shut; concealing the blaster pistol case.

She couldn't quite explain—even to herself—why she had done it.

Not even as she rose up to her feet and looked down on the cowering Fiona.

―――――――――

Before Louise could do anything else, she found herself getting thrown out of the room.

A doctor from the Infirmary had ordered everyone unnecessary from the suite.

At a loose end, and unsure whether or not Fiona would have anything useful to say in any case, Louise made her way along the hallway, headed for the lifts. It was only when she got to the lift that she noticed Niu standing on her heels. Louise glanced back at her, brow furrowed.

"I'm just going to get some air—think things through."

Niu tilted her head to one side. "That's fine," she replied, "but my orders are to accompany you."

"Fine," Louise shot back. "Where to now?"

Niu stuck her finger into her earpiece. She communicated with somebody, and then looked back at Louise. "That's up to you."

"Up to me *how?*" she replied. "You came for me, brought me to this suite so that I could offer a helping hand. Why don't you save us some time . . ." She took a deep breath, told herself to calm down. "What about Costantino Zito, his son; do they know about this?"

Niu shook her head. "They've been assigned to another Guardian, and their own Security personnel."

"For their own protection, I presume?"

Although Niu didn't so much as twitch, Louise was certain that a shine passed over the surface of her eyes.

"So," Louise continued, "I suppose I'm meant to just go right back to my bedroom . . . to wait till this thing is *over?*"

Niu said nothing at all.

"And what if I want to go to the Crescent Gardens?"

Niu reached up, stuck her finger into her earpiece once again. Her eyes returned to Louise. "That would be fine—the zone's been given the All-Clear."

"All right, then," Louise replied. "Let's go *there.*"

Without another word, they stepped into the lift and headed for the Lunar Grand lobby.

31

TERMINATION PROCEDURE

jhay set about packing up his things.

His microscope, the one he had brought up with him from Earth.

Next, he lifted the plastic box containing the memory sticks.

As he lifted them, they rattled together.

All of them held various dumps of his research in case there was some failure with the Link up here, on the Moon. He had got his research signed off by Mackenzie Angliss herself once he had agreed to her request—the one which asked him to choose between his life's work and—what might've proven to be—his life's love.

Finally, of course, there was the gilt-framed printed photograph.

It featured himself and his grandfather on his graduation day. The two of them grinned out from the frame. He recalled how his mother had told him that the photograph was too 'precious' for him to take up to the Moon; on such a fraught, dangerous voyage.

But, since Njhay looked at the photograph every single morning without fail, it would've been simply too heart-wrenching to be parted from it for the length of his rotation; for eighteen-months.

This rotation, though, as it had turned out, wouldn't last as long as he had believed.

The conditions, as they'd been worked out with Angliss, were fair.

In exchange for his cooperation in leaving the Celestial Stays Dome quietly, she would guarantee him a selection of glowing references along with a feasible and balanced explanation for the early termination of his contract.

It was more than Njhay could've hoped for.

And he supposed he should be thankful.

So why did he feel as if somebody had hollowed out his chest?

Why did it feel as if someone had torn out his heart?

. . . Why did this feel like the greatest mistake of his *life*?

As he set his personal effects down on one of the metal examination tables, he realised that he could hear approaching footsteps in the corridor outside.

How many times, while he'd skulked about here, busy with his lab work, had those footsteps sent shudders up his spine?

. . . That jarring—*knowing*—sensation that he was soon to be interrupted.

That his mind would soon be distracted from his work.

On Earth—*when he got back to Earth*—he resolved to pick out a place where he would be guaranteed peace and quiet; where he could keep the outside world at bay.

And where he wouldn't ever need to allow another person into his head . . . or his *heart*.

The footsteps grew louder.

Njhay adjusted his glasses across the bridge of his nose then turned his attention to the doorway.

He wondered if this would be someone having come to gloat; that he was finally getting chucked off the face of the Moon. Although he was hesitant to think that he had made enemies, he knew for a fact that there were those who would breathe a sigh of relief at his departure; and they'd hope his replacement would be willing to play the game.

He judged the footfall as insistent, undoubtedly *feminine* . . . but not belonging to Mackenzie Angliss—thank *God*.

When Louise appeared in the doorway, looking *extremely* dour-faced, he expected the worst.

He wondered if Mackenzie Angliss had decided against handing him forgiveness and was now, instead, going to dishonourably discharge him from his contract with Celestial Stays. But if that was the case then it seemed a strange messenger for her to send.

Why *Louise*?

At first, Louise flashed a smile at him, her eyes lighting up when they settled on his. However, her eyes soon shifted onto the boxes of his possessions.

In that moment, he realised what it must look like . . . well, it must look *a lot* like the truth. He broke from where he stood, reaching out for her.

But she evaded his grasp.

"What's this?" she said, looking back at him. "What's going *on*?"

He couldn't find the words for the longest time. He wondered if it was fear—if he was suddenly *struck dumb* because Louise frightened him . . .

Or was it simply because this felt so *wrong*?

How could this truly be happening?

Before he could say anything at all, Louise beat him to the punch.

Her beautiful, sapphire eyes rose to meet his.

"You're leaving?" she said, her voice impossibly fragile.

He wanted to deny it—more than *anything else* he wanted to say that it wasn't true.

But he realised he couldn't go against the truth.

He knew he could explain the choice of head over heart all day long, and yet it would never make sense to her . . . it would never make sense to *him* . . .

He opened his mouth to speak, but Louise was already retreating from the lab. She was heading out into the corridor. He watched on as she shook her head, mumbling something under her breath.

But he couldn't hear her.

And, after a brief, final glance, she slipped out of sight.

He was alone again . . . his life's work summed up in a microscope, a box of memory sticks and a framed portrait of himself and his grinning *dead* grandfather.

3 2

PROTOCOL BREACH

*O*n *her way to the exit* of the Crescent Gardens, Louise had the greatest of urges to smash the plants which sprouted from either side of the path. She wanted some way to express her anger. She wanted *everyone* to know just how she felt.

And what would be more notable than an act of sabotage on that which her lover—*ex-lover?*—Njhay had strived so hard to create?

It was hard to believe that, throughout the encounter, Niu had been present—albeit hidden from Njhay's sight, out in the corridor.

Perhaps that was why Louise had managed to restrain herself . . . maybe that was why she had kept herself from ripping him limb-from-limb.

As she quickened her pace, heading through the greenery of the Gardens, with Niu never far away, she wondered if there were any decent men left in existence; either down on Earth or up here, on the Moon.

Costantino Zito seemed the only specimen . . . and he was old enough to be her grandpa.

While she stormed toward the PEAR landing strip—with no destination in mind—she noticed some motion at the periphery of her vision. To begin with, she was certain that it would be Wendy, or Mackenzie Angliss. Either one of them come along to calm her down. No doubt, they would then inform her that it was good for her 'career' that she put her relationship with Njhay behind her. However, it wasn't either Mackenzie or Wendy.

It was Kyra.

Kyra Singh.

Louise was more taken aback by *who* it was than anything else.

She locked onto Kyra's wide, beautiful eyes and dared her to try and tell her something she didn't want to hear right now. Kyra, it seemed, spent the majority of her existence attempting to avoid contact—*conversation*—with Louise.

What was so important which necessitated a breach in standard-operating protocol now?

"Louise," Kyra said. "You're looking for one of your guests —aren't you?"

Louise felt her chest tighten.

Her heart skittered in her throat.

And her blood ran hot.

"Where is he?" she replied, her voice cool.

Kyra gave a slight smile, and then gestured to speak together off to one side . . . apparently out of Niu's earshot.

"It's fine," Louise said. "She's my shadow for the day."

Kyra shifted a glance at Niu, and then leaned in closer to Louise. "It's just," she said, "I would prefer she didn't hear."

"Why?"

"Because"—Kyra looked around, then stared long and hard at

Niu—"it may or may not involve something I shouldn't have been doing."

"What *were* you doing?"

Kyra clamped her eyes shut. "Like I said, I'd like to talk to you alone."

Louise glanced back at Niu. "Do you mind giving us a few minutes?"

Niu remained straight-faced. "My orders are to maintain a minimum of ten metres."

"Ten metres would be fine."

For a few moments, they stood in a sort of standoff, working out who was going to be the one to move away. In the end, it was Louise who trod away with Kyra.

They walked along the dug-out flowerbeds of the Gardens.

Every so often, Louise would dip down to inspect some flower or another; speculate about what its scientific name might be, and, most likely, get it wrong . . . if only to herself.

"Listen," Kyra said, her eyes glancing out ahead. "You need to promise you won't tell *anyone*."

"Okay," Louise replied, and felt like adding in a shrug for good measure, only abandoning the gesture at the last minute.

Kyra sighed. "I'm a journalist," she said.

Louise squinted at her. "You told me that already."

"No, you're not understanding—I'm *here*, on the *Moon*, on assignment . . . for a media outlet."

It took a second for this to sink in.

"You're sniffing out stories?" Louise said.

"You could say that."

"Dished up anything good?"

"Look," she continued, "all you need to know is that I happened to be skulking about the Armstrong Archive when I noticed a folder which'd been pulled."

"A 'folder' ?"

"Yeah, you know, made of cardboard—filled with sheets of paper."

"*Yeah*, I know what a *folder* is . . . but I didn't realise there were paper records."

Kyra shrugged. "There's all sorts there—you've just got to do some digging."

"And what about this *folder*?"

Kyra glanced over Louise's shoulder, again looking to Niu following; strictly observing the established ten-metre periphery. "Well, it had plans within it."

"Plans of *what?*"

She shifted a glance back at Louise. "Of the Lunar Caverns."

"And what does this have to do with the missing guest?" She paused, recalling that Mackenzie and Wendy had said that not speaking his name would only give him power. "What does this have to do with *Alex Barn?*"

"This is the part that could get me into trouble . . . When I performed an illicit scan on the records—*on the Link*—I found out that it was Alex Barn who checked out the folder."

Louise was so swept up with this whole discovery that she didn't think to ask after Kyra's interest in Alex Barn; or for her *reason* in being at the Armstrong Archive at all . . . surely *well* out of her jurisdiction. Then again, from what she'd said, it didn't seem that Kyra was entirely on the surface of the Moon to serve Celestial Stays.

"Look, it's my best guess," Kyra replied, "that Alex Barn's in the Lunar Caverns."

Louise felt a shifting sensation in her gut.

It seemed as if a large weight laid down on her shoulders.

She thought about the Lunar Caverns—and that unforgettable night she and Njhay had shared . . . but Njhay was gone . . . or he soon would be . . .

And what did it really matter *where* Alex Barn was?

She could pass this information on now.

Wash her hands of it.

She turned back to Kyra. "Thanks," she said, managing a smile.

Kyra managed a vague smile in return. "It's just a hunch—I don't know if anything will come of it; but it might be a place to start." She held still for a long time, shifted a glance over to Niu, apparently suspicious about whether or not she'd overheard any of the information. Finally, she looked back at Louise. "My secret'll be safe with you, I hope?"

Louise nodded. "Don't worry."

Kyra shifted away, heading toward the exit. "Good luck," she said, over her shoulder.

And then—just like that—Louise was alone.

It was all on her.

To track down Alex Barn.

THE LUNAR CAVERNS

lthough Louise hadn't wanted anything of the sort—hadn't wanted anything more to do with this 'lockdown', or this *'search'*, however it was being termed—she found herself being roped into the search party going through the Caverns.

Thankfully, though, she wasn't expected to enter the Caverns herself.

So she stayed to the periphery.

Niu remained as watchful as ever, her hand continuing to linger over her holstered blaster pistol.

As Louise stood and stared at the opening of the Lunar Caverns, she couldn't help but cast her mind back to Kyra; to the information she'd dealt her.

If there had been one real enigma throughout her time beneath the Celestial Stays Dome—beside *Njhay*—it had been Kyra.

Now, though, she had given Louise a glimpse of what she was really about.

And the mystery had only thickened.

She watched on as the Security team—dressed in their black overalls and fitted with mobile force fields—trudged in and out of the Caverns. Each time she saw a silhouette against the interior tunnel light, she expected to see Alex's face as he was restrained by a pair of Security personnel.

But—*each and every time*—there was no sign of Alex at all.

It slowly got through to Louise that while Kyra had been right to share her hunch, that was all it had been. In the end, there'd been no substance to the suspicion, and they would need to move on; to search the next possible location.

On their way to the Caverns, Niu had become strangely talkative.

To begin with, she had detailed the exact rendering of the night's events, as they had been related to Security by witnesses in adjoining suites.

There had been some sort of a disturbance—that explained the bruise on Fiona's cheek—followed by the breakage, the *tossing* of several items.

That explained the state of the hotel room.

By the time Niu had shown up on the scene, she had found Fiona in her catatonic state, unwilling to cooperate with anyone .. . and that was the point when Niu had decided to call Louise, *before* calling in a heavy-handed Security team.

Niu also went on to explain that nobody—*none of the medical staff*—had got any information out of Fiona as pertaining to Alex's whereabouts.

Niu opened up to Louise about the various surveillance measures which the Dome counted on to keep an eye on its guests; or—as she termed it—the measures in place to keep guests 'safe'.

She went on to tell Louise that Alex Barn had managed to evade each and every one of these measures. To begin with, he had logged off the Link, making it so that he could no longer be tracked by the Dome database. He had shown up on the basic security cameras, of course, but then he had somehow disappeared once he'd left the Lunar Grand.

It was a true mystery for the entire Security team, although, as Louise observed, it wasn't one which they weren't taking some enjoyment out of . . . she supposed that Security's brief—for the most part—extended to breaking up drunken arguments and shepherding the more-adventurous of the guests back to their hotel rooms when they'd gone on an ill-advised afternoon 'stroll' and got themselves hopelessly lost.

Throughout the conversation, Niu had also instructed Louise to address her by her first name—*Lan* . . . and despite their relationship not really moving much past the level of scant acquaintances, Louise had to admit that, by the end of the journey in the PEAR, she'd started to feel a little more at ease in *Lan's* company.

Still, if Louise hadn't had other things on her mind—notably the location of her borderline insane ex-lover—then she might've registered it further.

Louise felt herself drift away until she noted a member of the Security team emerge from the entrance of the Caverns. He was a man with white hair, bristling biceps—even beneath his overalls. He had a hardened, leathery complexion.

If anybody was on their final lunar rotation, then it must've been him.

She also caught sight of the glistening, golden Supervisor's badge sewn onto his breast pocket.

He held a helmet beneath his arm, in a way which Louise could quite easily picture as belonging in some science-fiction, action-adventure film.

She also caught sight of the red-and-white flag with a Maple Leaf at its centre.

Apparently having already isolated Louise for some kind of special attention, he strode toward her. His expression was stern, though his eyes were quick in their sockets, surely ready for Alex to leap out of the shadows at a moment's notice.

"Supervisor William Duval," he declared, thrusting his hand out at Louise.

She took it off him, feeling as if she might be somewhat lucky to have survived the handshake. "Louise Williams," she replied, and then, catching herself, added, "*Guardian* Louise Williams."

Duval grunted. "My team have scoured the Caverns, but there's no sign of your guest."

Louise didn't much like the blaming tone; the idea that this was *her* guest and nobody else's . . . that she was responsible in some way. Then again, this man seemed as if he had some sort of a military background, and in that world there was *always* somebody to blame—usually the one who was one notch up on the totem pole.

She glanced to Lan, and then back to Duval. "What now, then?" she said.

Duval grimaced. "That's the question . . . I suppose we slip the perimeter back . . . take it from there. See if we can't get a better idea of where he's got to." He reached up, scratched at his thinning white hair. "We'll let you know of any updates."

And with that, Duval strode away.

Louise was on the cusp of doing the same—*leaving the scene behind*—when she heard somebody calling her name.

For several long seconds, she felt her blood freezing.

Her thoughts seemed to stick in her brain.

Everything moved slowly.

Just for a second—*that one second*—she imagined that it might be Alex . . . that he had shown up here, outside the Lunar Caverns; somehow having evaded the Security team.

But, when Louise properly absorbed just who it was, she felt as if her heart might melt . . . all over again.

Njhay.

Njhay García.

She took him in very slowly, from those bronze-green eyes, to those unruly, black corkscrew curls. And then she remembered her anger. How she had flashed with fury not more than an hour earlier. How could she forget?

She turned her back to him, and stalked toward the PEAR landing strip.

She heard him following on her heels; advancing on her quickly.

She broke into a run—*determined* to outpace him.

As she closed on the landing strip, she watched on as a PEAR descended from out of the sky, its spherical pod promising a way-out for her; a chance for her to get away from Njhay for good.

To never see him again for so long as she lived.

She was only a matter of steps away from the PEAR—its visor peeling back to reveal the slick interior—when she felt Njhay grab hold of her overall sleeve.

His strength was firm but there was no fury there.

No lack of control.

Not like Alex.

Gripping her sleeve tightly, he gently turned her around so that she faced him.

So that the two of them stared at one another—*eyeball to eyeball*.

She breathed in his fresh, minty breath.

As he inhaled deeply, she watched his pectoral muscles rise and fall.

There was something intrinsically *rhythmic* about him.

Something which spoke to her—lightly, but *fiercely*—'Force of Nature'.

"Louise," he said, his voice husky, as if he was on the cusp of asking a question.

Although every thought in her mind told her to yank herself free, to get into the PEAR which'd just landed nearby, her body wouldn't obey.

Somehow she knew that the two of them were deeply connected in a way which—*quite simply*—wouldn't allow them to be parted. That had to be the explanation, hadn't it?

She felt her chest rising and falling against her overalls. It seemed as if her mind might overpower her; that she would, at last, come to her senses.

See that she could be just as happy—just as *fulfilled*—if she made the conscious choice now never to allow another to get close to her . . . never to allow another to *hurt* her.

It surprised her to see that he was smiling. "I made my choice," he said. "I've *made* my choice."

Louise stared back into his eyes, still unable to understand. "*What* choice?" she replied.

"I'm going to stay."

Needles pricked the surface of her skin. She felt the tiniest bolt of lightning tickle her heart. Her mind was lost for several seconds. She wondered if she would ever get it back.

"But, your work . . ."

Already Njhay was shaking his head. "It doesn't matter —*nothing* matters . . . although I've resisted it for so long—although I thought I could fight it; now I know better. That it was all in vain. That I have a responsibility—a *need*—to see this through . . . to see where the two of us will end up." When he stared at her now, she saw that there were tears clinging to the surface of his eyes. "Anything else would be to violate something beautiful—*something natural*—before it ever got a chance of coming into being." He paused for long moment and Louise could see how—as a man of science—he was wrestling to find his sense of the fantastical; of the metaphorical. "Like clipping a flower bud before it has the chance to bloom."

She couldn't help but feel a sly smile creep onto her lips. "We'll work on those poetics of yours," she said, "but I appreciate the sentiment."

Eyes locked—one on the other—they kissed softly.

And long.

34

PROXIMITY ALARM

*L*ouise woke with a start.

She peered out into the darkness.

Like parted waves of a frothing, inky-black sea, she expected it to come tumbling in on her at a moment of its choosing. To crush her with its almighty power.

To drag out every last breath from her lungs . . .

She caught her bearings, feeling the mattress beneath her.

She reminded herself where she was.

In her room; in the Basements.

As she reached up to rub at her temples, she thought about how it was any wonder that she had managed to drift off to sleep . . . that at a time so fraught with tension she had managed to slip away into the land of dreams.

She turned.

Saw him lying there.

Njhay.

His chest rising and falling with his rhythmic breathing.

Taking care not to stir him, she slipped out of bed, picked her way carefully across the room to the bathroom. She poured herself a glass of water; tipped it down her throat with the liquid hardly even touching the inside of her mouth.

Just straight into her body, like plugging herself into an IV drip.

The glass made a slight *clink* when she set it down.

She had been neglecting her basic needs throughout this whole ordeal; not getting enough to eat or drink. The situation had been going on for over twelve hours now; the whole Dome had been placed on 'lockdown' . . . the Security team prowled the perimeter; searching for Alex.

Wondering if they had had any success, she reached up for her earpiece and pressed; channelling her thoughts with the Link, trying to find out any information she could.

Nothing.

. . . Or at least, she had received no communication from them.

Who was she, really, to expect to be kept updated on the chase?

She who had only been made a Guardian to 'keep up appearances' for Costantino Zito's visit.

Still, she couldn't help but feel that the Security team held her responsible for 'her' guest.

Was that what was making her so anxious?

With a deep breath in, and then a long exhale out, Louise decided that she needed to take a walk.

That she needed to leave behind the stuffy air of her bedroom.

She half thought about waking Njhay, having him come along with her so she wouldn't have to feel alone. But he looked so at peace—so *deeply* asleep—that she decided against it.

Her focus shifted to the wallpaper, to the dark black clouds which drifted by.

No wonder she had had those looming, terrifying dreams of

waves crashing down upon her . . . driving her down to the seabed where she would remain forever more.

Perhaps she should speak with whoever was responsible for the automated wallpaper programming; asking them if it might be possible to choose a more calming assortment of images.

When Louise asked for permission to leave her room, she expected to be denied.

It took her slightly aback when the door simply slid free of its place.

Once out in the corridor, however, she was met with a stern—if a little *sleep-deprived*—"Halt!"

A tingle ran up her spine.

At first, she suspected the worst . . . though how Alex had managed to get into the Basements without required authorisation —how he might've got through the force field without being on the receiving end of *several* nasty burns—escaped her.

But her heart soon slowed its beating.

Lan emerged from the shadows.

Her hand lingering over the blaster pistol strapped to her thigh.

Seeing it was Louise, her features softened. "What're you doing up and about at this time?"

Louise stared back at Lan. "I . . . had a bad dream."

And—even as she said it—she couldn't help but feel like she was just some young girl getting up to bother her parents with some nonsense detail.

Lan, though, if she did feel that Louise was being somewhat silly, said nothing by way of response. She only said, "My orders are for you to remain in your room until further notice—until the guest has been apprehended."

Louise held herself very still. "I was just wondering if it was possible to . . . uh"—here she paused, knowing she was about to sound like an idiot—"I'd like to *return* to the Lunar Caverns—"

"Out of the question."

Louise stayed silent for several moments, wondering just how much she would feel confident about sharing. In the end, she decided that she had nothing to lose.

From what she had picked up on, the Security team was at an almost complete loss as to what to do next . . . as to how they might go about tracking down Alex Barn.

"I think I know where he is," Louise added, finally—*firmly*. "Somewhere you haven't looked."

Lan eyed her closely. "Then let us know—we'll flush him out."

Louise shook her head. She wondered why she hadn't told Security before about the empty blaster pistol case she'd uncovered in the suite. She decided that it was because she'd been afraid they might hurt him; that they might *kill* him . . . and for whatever reason Louise had run from him—for whatever damage he might've dealt her—she couldn't face the idea of him coming to harm if it could be at all prevented.

And certainly not when she was so inextricably linked to his disappearance in the first place.

Now, though, Louise saw that it would be the only way of possibly enlisting Lan's help. "I've got the feeling he might be armed; that he won't come quietly . . . not if he's faced with force on our side. I don't want anyone to get hurt if it can be helped."

Lan looked away now, apparently considering this angle. No doubt she had strong feelings about having fellow Security team members coming to harm when it could be prevented; having *friends* come to harm when it could be prevented.

When Louise breathed in and felt her whole body shuddering as if reacting against the air, she forced the feeling away; *forced* herself to remain strong. "He needs someone who he knows to go in and talk him out . . ."

Lan gave Louise a steely glare. "His fiancée's in no fit state for that—"

"I mean *me*," Louise replied, a touch more bile in her response than she had intended.

They slipped into silence.

Finally, Lan spoke up. "Word from Duval is that nobody is to go in or come out of the Caverns. No exceptions. They've got shooters fixed on the tunnel entrance for whenever he rears his head."

"But surely *you* can find a way in?"

Lan remained straight-faced for a long, long time.

Louise was certain she was going to deny her this opportunity.

But then Lan relented, her cheekbones retreating up her face.

Her frown replaced by a slight smile.

35

RESTRICTED ACCESS

ouise was surprised when Lan didn't program the trajectory of the PEAR for the Lunar Caverns but for the Stellar Tide Casino.

Louise's first thought, of course, was that she had been betrayed; that Lan had decided against disobeying her superior's orders . . . that would've been in keeping with Louise's first impression of Lan. However, instead of Louise finding herself surrounded by a whole host of Security team members, pumping her for information on the whereabouts of Alex Barn, Lan led Louise past the smiling host at the welcome desk and down a tight staircase.

The whole time—despite Lan's no-nonsense black overalls clearly marking her out as a member of the Security team—Louise expected someone to appear out of the woodwork to stop them.

But they kept on going . . . down and down and *down* . . .

Finally, when Louise estimated they had to be a good five or six levels beneath the lunar surface, and into almost complete pitch-black, Lan turned to her and held something out for her to take.

"Here," she said. "This should help."

In the near darkness, it took Louise a couple of seconds to identify the object which'd been thrust into her hands. Finally she realised what it was.

An illumination stick.

She turned it over, glanced back at Lan, still a touch confused about just what was going on.

Lan explained.

"Head on along the tunnel here," she said, indicating the passageway, steeped in darkness. "It'll bring you out into a narrow branch off one of the main caverns. Just follow it back." She gave Louise the hint of a smile then nodded at the illumination stick. "I'm sorry I only have one of those; didn't exactly have any advance warning and we only get one through standard issue. If I was you, I'd save it up till you really need it . . . till the dark *really* starts to get to you."

Still feeling stunned at what had just transpired, she turned back to Lan, her mind almost dizzy with the many questions humming through her head. "How did you . . . find out about *this* route?"

Lan tapped the side of her nose.

Smiled.

And then turned away from Louise.

"Good luck," she said. "And one piece of advice."

Louise stared back at her through the near darkness. "What?"

"When you come back out—through the main exit to the Caverns—make sure your hands are where the Security team can see them." She turned away, heading back up the staircase, toward the surface and the Stellar Tide Casino. "Don't want anybody getting their face shot off or anything."

And—with that merry thought on her mind—Louise trod on.

Into the darkness.

Louise couldn't help but feel her thoughts turning back to her dream; to those inky-black waves coming pummelling down upon her.

As she walked, she reached out and brushed the side of the tunnel, finding some reassurance that she was headed in the direction which Lan had indicated.

The tunnel itself, as she had soon discovered, wasn't all that wide.

When she reached out her arms, she could feel both sides.

When she stretched up, her fingertips brushed the ceiling. A little of the lunar dust sprinkled down. It reminded Louise of a time when she'd gone to stay with her grandmother during the summer. Her grandmother had lived out in the countryside, near a large lake. She'd had a great, big wooden house with lots and lots of rooms. One day, Louise had become curious and she'd ventured up to one of the attic rooms. She recalled how she'd stridden through the rooms feeling the dust puffing up against her cheeks . . . almost tickling her . . . as if there was some sort of benevolent, hidden force. That was how Louise felt now.

She felt *almost* as if something was guiding her.

Encouraging her to make peace with her past.

Once and for all.

And what was a fear of death when placed alongside that?

Louise strode on into the darkness, clutching the unlit illumination stick, biding her time . . . telling herself not to waste it when she finally did activate the device.

Several times, Louise's earpiece informed her that she had gone out of range of the Link; that she had lost her connection to the Dome.

Becoming tired that each time the Link came back online, it struck those even, half dozen chimes of the Celestial Stays Dome, she switched her earpiece off for good. It was a strange feeling, to be striding through this tunnel, no doubt hundreds of metres beneath the lunar surface, and to be entirely cut off from every-thing—from *everyone* else.

Finally, she felt a change in gradient beneath her feet. She could tell that she was now on an upward slope, headed back toward the lunar surface.

And hopefully up to the Lunar Caverns.

Acting on impulse, she reached out ahead. Her fingertips brushed bare rock. It sent a shudder through her body; a thrill down to the pit of her stomach. She drew in a breath—feeling that the air was thinner here; that it would be easy to get a head rush if she went on too quickly; if she didn't respect her body's limitations.

She continued up into the passageway.

When she felt the walls of the tunnel retreat from her, she decided that—now her guidance was gone—there would be no choice but for her to utilise the illumination stick.

So she did so.

Her surroundings immediately lit up with the cool, bluish glow.

She made out the silhouettes of the rocks surrounding her.

The darkness up ahead slowly becoming stripped back with every one of her steps.

And Alex Barn somewhere *out there*.

Once she had caught onto her bearings, she worked out the location of the main chamber of the Lunar Caverns. Then she began to follow it back toward the entrance.

As she trod along, she took care to breathe in deeply, to keep her lungs filled.

One thing was for certain.

She wouldn't give up now.

She wouldn't *give in* now.

Without so much as a conscious thought about it, she located the tunnel leading off from the main cavern; the tunnel which had been marked to expand the Caverns.

The tunnel down which Njhay had led her.

This, she was convinced, was where she would locate Alex.

And his blaster pistol.

Louise quickened her pace, feeling the steady, blue glow of the illumination stick sending the shadows scurrying for the corners of the tunnel. When she got to the dead-end, the place where Njhay had set out that mattress, and the tea lights . . . the rose petals . . . Louise couldn't help but feel herself being whisked back. To those shudders of pleasure. To those warming *happy* times.

It was almost impossible to fathom that she and Alex had ever shared anything similar, although, she knew it had to be true. How else might she have fallen for him?

She stood still in the centre of the cave for several moments, simply shining the light about the area, searching for what she'd seen, lying on her back, when she had come around . . . just before she and Njhay had been discovered. When she'd thought this lunar dream might all be over.

She located it.

The *hole*.

Halfway up the wall.

She peered into the blackness, wondering if it *was* truly possible. If that hole really was large enough for a human being to fit through; even one as slippery and adept as Alex Barn . . .

She supposed the Security team had been thorough with their search of the Caverns and that they too had come upon this hole. Perhaps they had drawn the same conclusion as Louise was doing now . . . that someone surely *couldn't* squeeze through.

There was only one way for her to find out.

She thrust the illumination stick into the waistband of her overalls and then helped herself up onto the pieces of rock which jutted out from the wall. She moved slowly and took immense care to find her balance before moving onto the next support.

When she finally felt her fingertips grip the edge of the hole, she sank her teeth into her lower lip, tasting blood as she hoiked herself upward.

It was hard for her brain to convince her stomach that she had truly arrived. That she was now lying on her belly, staring into the depths of the hole stretching out ahead of her. She couldn't tell how it worked; if it became tighter still as it went along. Only now did Louise realise she hadn't so much as told Lan where she suspected Alex to be located.

It could well be that Alex wasn't here at all, and that Louise would find herself stuck halfway along . . . and that nobody would hear her crying out for help . . . well, *ever*.

But she threw off the negative thoughts, telling herself that she couldn't afford to allow them to enter her mind. She needed to keep going. She needed to keep on pushing herself forward . . . because—if she ever stopped going forward—then she really *would* become stuck.

On her belly, she slithered her way along the tunnel, taking hold of the pieces of rock—using them to grip and hoist her way through.

Each minute movement sapped her energy and there came a point when she was certain she wouldn't be able to go on . . . but she forced herself . . . *implored* herself . . .

If she ever wanted to escape—*truly escape*—then now was the time.

Now was the time to show her strength.

Finally, she felt the area opening up around her . . . the walls of the Caverns seeming almost to retreat. When she reached up above her head, she realised that the ceiling had retreated, and that, indeed, there was now room enough for her to stand.

She eased herself up gently, taking care to check her balance.

Hands shaking, she reached into her waistband and withdrew the illumination stick.

She held it up straight, again relegating the darkness to the shadows.

She peered out ahead.

And then she saw him.

Slumped up.

Eyes closed.

Head bowed over his chest.

Blaster pistol clenched tightly in his fist.

Her whole body tensed.

She gripped the illumination stick tighter.

And then—with a futile glimmer—its light went out.

THE HIDDEN TOMB

Louise's heart leaped up in her throat.

The air tasted salty when she breathed in—thick with *sulphur?*

Her mind became stuck on a single track.

Dead, dead, dead . . . he's dead!

The darkness seemed to reach out its cold, damp touch, brushing its fingertips up against her skin, bringing every hair to attention.

And then she heard his voice.

"Louise," he said. "I thought you'd never come."

He sounded tired—*weary*—as if he had fought the longest battle and he was looking forward to a period of rest and relaxation; of some well-earned time at her side.

She held herself still.

Too afraid to move.

The darkness was complete.

She wondered if Alex had been here so long that *he* could see in the black.

Her question was quickly answered. There was an almost unnoticeable flicker of a tiny orange light. This was soon followed by a bright-yellow flash; a new, steady light flooding the Caverns.

It took her a moment or two to realise that the light came from the blaster pistol; the one which Alex was clutching so tightly.

She held up her forearm to shield her eyes from the glare.

She was half conscious of his silhouette rising off the tunnel floor.

She observed him support himself with the wall.

Get to his feet.

He staggered to one side a couple of times, but eventually found his balance.

And his eyes—like sharpened daggers—peered out.

He pointed the blaster pistol at her chest.

Gave her a wicked smile.

"All this time," Alex said, "I've been thinking—turning things over . . . working out how we might do things going forward."

Even with the pistol pointed at her, she felt something deep within reject this out of hand. She shook her head. "What do you mean 'going forward'? There is *no* going forward—not for us."

Alex cocked his head to one side. His eyelids drooped in a sleepy fashion. Now her eyes had better adjusted to the bright light, she saw that his burgundy-coloured guest overalls had become snagged and torn . . . no doubt her own overalls were in a similar state following her own progress through the Caverns.

Alex took a step toward her. "You really were perfect, Louise." Apparently sensing his intimidating movements, he checked himself, pausing. "We might have lived *forever*—together—in perfect *luxury*." He smiled wider still. "An *unbreakable* team."

"No," Louise replied, her voice firm, proud.

Decided.

"It's all just a fantasy."

Alex's expression fell slightly at this observation. "A 'fantasy' ?" he replied, as if perplexed by this notion.

Louise nodded back at him.

Alex seemed to become introspective, almost as if he was examining his own position; what he had done . . . what he was doing now . . . to be on the run, on the Moon . . . just what did he believe he could achieve?

There was a long moment of silence between the two of them.

Louise felt a prickling sensation pass over the surface of her skin.

She had the urge to scratch, but she resisted.

"I want *you*," Alex continued, breaking the silence, "to come with *me*; back to Earth. And I want things to be just like they were."

Only now did she fully comprehend his tone; the fact that he was—apparently—close to tears. She glanced about her, as if there might be someone lurking in the shadows, witnessing this faceoff . . . though, of course, there was no one.

She stared back into Alex's eyes, hoping he would understand.

That she could *make* him understand.

"That's impossible," she said, finally.

Alex took stock of her response and then advanced toward her. Another few steps and he would be close enough to touch her. If his desire—with that blaster pistol; with this whole *routine* of his— had been to intimidate her, then he had fully succeeded.

He closed the gap.

He held the blaster down at his hip.

Pointed to her gut.

Louise shut her eyes, expecting the shot to come. When it failed to do so, she opened them again.

She was surprised to see that Alex now held the blaster pistol to his temple.

Her lips moved but no sound came out.

Later she wondered if there was something deep within her which called—which *demanded*—his death . . . some unshakable voice which would not be quietened; no matter how Louise attempted to silence it with rationalisation and *reason*.

She watched on—in slow motion—as he squeezed the trigger.

37

RECOVERY

Louise stood outside the Lunar Caverns.

Just as trauma victims were treated back on Earth, she had been given a foil blanket—a 'space blanket' as it was appropriately named. The warmth made her feel just a little less likely to faint.

As she stood by, with Security streaming in and out of the Caverns, she remained entranced. She wanted to see for herself when they brought out the body bag.

When they brought him all wrapped up.

Done.

Dead.

On the day of Alex Barn's death, she had believed that her heart would ache; that she would feel a frozen void opening up within her chest. She had believed that, she too, would've felt close to death. But quite the opposite was true.

In truth, though, she really felt nothing at all.

Supervisor Duval barked orders to his charges as they went

about their work. Among the many faces, Louise caught sight of Lan. The two of them made eye contact for a second. Louise caught a smile off her . . . nothing more than the briefest of flickers, but a *smile* all the same . . .

As she stood by—at the Caverns entrance—she felt someone draw up behind her.

She turned.

Saw who it was.

She might've guessed . . .

Njhay.

Although he looked wide awake now, she noted his bloodshot eyes and the more-ruffled-than-usual hair.

He stood stock-still—*staring at the Caverns*—as if there was something Security had missed.

Before he could say anything at all, Louise threw her arms about his midriff, pulled him into her.

Buried her face in his chest.

She felt his warmth. She breathed in his scent.

Blood pumped to her heart.

And she felt human again.

Finally, she channelled into what Njhay said. His voice was throaty and betrayed the rude-awakening he'd surely experienced not so long ago. "Is that . . . is that *him?*"

Louise felt her gut tighten.

She didn't want to turn around.

She didn't want to *look.*

She just wanted him to be *gone.*

She clung on tightly to Njhay, feeling as if he might try and prise himself free of her; that he might try to escape her clutches . . . that he somehow wouldn't stick to the promise which he had made; that he would stay with her, on the Moon.

Finally, though, Louise felt Njhay moving her about in his arms, turning her in the direction of the Caverns with great ease.

All she needed to do now was open her eyes.

So she did.

To begin with, she couldn't quite cope with the sight before her.

Four members of Security escorting Alex from the Lunar Caverns. She took in how Alex lay on a stretcher, how his body had been tucked up with a blanket, and how his face had been left uncovered. Motivated by some gruesome longing for knowledge, she searched his head for any sign of the blaster hole. It took her another moment to realise that there wasn't one at all.

Only a large, red welt.

Her eyes moved down slowly, to take in his covered body.

And she saw—*no mistake about it*—his chest rise and fall with the unmistakable movement of respiration.

Although Njhay insisted he take Louise back to the Basements, she resisted.

Perhaps it was just an adrenalin high, but she knew she wouldn't be able to summon the peace of mind drifting off to sleep would require.

In the end, she convinced Njhay to take her to the Crescent Gardens.

There was something about the sprawling vegetation—something about being amongst the *greenery*—which allowed her to breathe more easily; which allowed her some long-deserved peace and quiet . . .

And so, as she walked arm in arm with Njhay through the

Gardens, she allowed her mind to go limp . . . she gave herself permission to not think about anything at all.

Finally, when they'd reached the end of the Gardens, Louise couldn't help but turn into Njhay and say, "He's still alive —*isn't he?*"

Njhay said nothing.

"Why didn't the blaster shot kill him?"

Njhay held himself very still, and Louise felt the gentle throbbing of his heartbeat.

There was very little that could calm her right now, but a walk through the Crescent Gardens while being close to Njhay was one of those things.

"I suppose he had it set to STUN." Njhay looked past her, out through the sprawling vegetation and over the rest of the Dome, as if it was an enigma that would never be solved . . . at least not by him. "I don't understand what he wanted to do . . . why he went into the Caverns; what he hoped to achieve."

When Louise spoke, she felt weakness creeping into her voice for the first time. But she put effort into maintaining her tone . . . to not allowing it to crumple up. She had been strong for this long and she was determined to remain strong just a little longer; until she could find some place where she could be alone.

Where she could *cry.*

"He knew I'd come after him," Louise replied. "He *expected* me to follow him . . . and, quite honestly, there was nothing else to be done." She shook her head, followed Njhay's gaze as he looked off into the distance, over the Dome. "We spent a long time together, you need to remember that; we knew one another's mind . . . even after all this time." She paused again. "Perhaps he was hurt—maybe he needed a chance to say goodbye . . . and this was his way of doing so."

As if reading her mind, Njhay said nothing at all by way of response.

He only squeezed her a little tighter to his firm body.

Louise couldn't help but feel radiant at the prospect of their future.

Because now she had one.

38

DECORATION

*L*ouise *stumbled about her room*, trying to get herself into some kind of decent shape. She had been informed that she was to be decorated for . . . well, whatever it was that the Dome administration believed she had done.

In a way, she felt extremely guilty about all the pomp; how those higher-ups had made out what she'd done was some form of 'bravery'.

While, really, Louise had done it for no one but herself.

She had scoured her wardrobe three times over; and each time she had discarded each of the royal-blue overalls in turn. Not since she'd gone to school, and had been compelled to wear a uniform, had she believed that having a stringent dress code to adhere to might be a problem.

Whereas before—at school—she had frequently struggled for *some* way to set herself out against the mass of conformity; now she was searching for something along the lines of 'regal' . . . an outfit which might show that she was somehow *worthy* of this distinction she was about to receive.

And now she was thoroughly stuck.

Deciding that the only way forward was for her to take several steps back from the wardrobe, she slumped down on the edge of the bed. And then, because there was nobody to tell her different, she buried her face in her hands.

Maybe she would've cried if it hadn't been for the notification in her earpiece that there was somebody at the door.

Her mind was so fraught with what was to come, that she commanded the door open without even thinking about it . . . without considering that she wore only a towel; that she hadn't even had a chance to smudge on so much as eyeshadow or rake her hair up into some kind of order.

Louise was glad—if a little surprised—to find Alicia standing in the doorway.

And she was—quite frankly—*delighted* to note the bag which she held in her hands . . . and, more to the point, *excited* as to just what it might contain.

"All-righty," Alicia said, stepping into the room with a slight smile. "I come bearing gifts—gifts of *beauty*."

Louise remained sat on the edge of the bed, unable to move for the relief which coursed through her veins. She couldn't quite fathom an alternate reality where Alicia hadn't walked right through her bedroom door with all life's solutions in a neatly wrapped plastic bag.

It turned out to be the same garment as before.

If it had been any other occasion—any other *circumstance*—then Louise supposed she might've felt somewhat deflated . . . but given the very *special* nature of this particular garment; that it could change colour and pattern—*style*—as easily as any chameleon worth its skin, she was ecstatic.

Finally, Louise leaped free of her funk, landing with her feet a neat shoulders-width apart. She was already reaching out for the bag when Alicia explained that, *really*, they needed to do something about Louise's hair first.

With her hair well and truly 'done'; packed into tight, playful—and yet strangely *elegant*—ringlets; Alicia went to work fitting Louise for the dress.

In the end, Alicia picked out a sleek, simple double-strap design, with a square neck to show off Louise's cleavage. And though she clawed a couple of times at the neckline of her dress, Alicia finally won the battle, keeping Louise's hands from 'interfering'.

They settled on a royal-blue colour—in keeping with the Celestial Stays colour scheme—and then, everything apparently ready, they stood regarding one another . . . but mostly with Alicia regarding *Louise*.

"Who's going to be there?" Louise finally got out.

Alicia smiled back kindly. "From what I've heard it's going to be a fairly small affair—I think they're keen to play this down, though it shouldn't say anything about how highly they hold your work; what you've done." She smiled wider. "That's the hospitality game, I guess—the guests come and go, as is their whim." Her mouth formed an oh-shape, and she held up a finger. "There is at least *one* guest coming, though."

Louise flashed her eyebrows. "Who?"

"Costantino Zito," Alicia replied.

Louise's chest tightened.

Her gut sank.

"In fact," Alicia continued, "from what I hear, he wants to

congratulate you himself. When it was explained to him who eventually managed to reel Alex Barn in, there was no stopping him from attending the ceremony."

A tremble caught Louise.

Blood rushed to her temples.

She reached up to the bruise which Fiona had dealt her. It still protruded smartly from her forehead. She rubbed it a couple of times—as if it was some sort of good-luck charm.

"I really didn't do anything," Louise said. "The blaster—*well*, it was set to STUN before I even got there . . . even if he'd shot me I wouldn't have been killed . . . *he* knocked *himself* out."

Alicia's smile faltered.

Louise wondered if she'd said the wrong thing.

If there was now going to be a swift cancellation of the entire ceremony.

If Louise had exposed herself as a fraud.

Alicia leaned in close. "I suppose we've all got our secrets . . . what makes them count, though, is who we choose to tell."

With that, and a mysterious, unplaceable smile, she retreated from her.

Louise took a long few moments to absorb this.

She cast her mind back.

Something nagged at her.

Something.

The hotel suite . . . the bedside table . . . where Louise had discovered the blaster pistol . . . the takeaway box from the Orbital Café . . .

Her whole face must've been the picture of shock.

"Yes," Alicia said, "I *know* . . . I should've said something about the blaster when I delivered those goodies to their suite rather than just setting it to STUN . . . but there's something that you need to learn about Celestial Stays—*about life on the Moon*—and it's that, at all times, you need to cut the guests some slack; allow certain things to slip . . ."

"Except when they go running off on their own?"

"Yeah," Alicia agreed. "Anyway, I don't know about you, but I kind of like the story where you disarmed Barn, switched his gun to STUN then shot him in the head . . . what'd you think?"

Louise hadn't time to say anything by way of response because Alicia wasn't done yet.

"And I kind of *also* like the story of how you managed—*without any outside help at all*—to steal your way into the Lunar Caverns . . . despite it being under constant surveillance."

Here, as if to push home the point further, Alicia winked.

Louise's jaw latched open.

"*Or,*" Alicia went on, her tone rising further, "that you *knew* to check out the Lunar Caverns at all . . ." Here Alicia finally trailed off, and Louise assumed this to be the end of the revelations.

It was true to say that Louise had had the help of Kyra, Lan, and, of course, Alicia.

Without any one of them, she would never have been able to track down Alex . . . and, worse, she might've ended up *dead*.

Somehow, Louise managed to squeeze out a shaky reply. "Thank you. Thanks to *all* of you."

Alicia batted this away as a cat might a ball of wool. "Don't mention it—girls've got to look out for one another, especially on the frontiers of human civilisation."

As Louise ventured out of her room, she was met by Lan; dressed as usual in her black overalls.

Without a word, Lan reached out and took hold of Louise's hand; giving it a good, firm shake. "Congratulations, Guardian Williams. I'm here as your personal guard—to make sure you reach the ceremony okay."

Still feeling stunned at this treatment, she smiled back. "Good to know I'm in safe hands."

Lan nodded in reply, then with a firm *snap* of the heel, led the way to the PEAR landing strip.

Louise had to admit that she *wasn't* all that surprised to find Kyra Singh standing there.

She was taken *more* off guard when Kyra leaped into her, embracing her tightly.

And taken off guard further still when Kyra stood back and beamed at her . . . by far the most brilliant smile which Kyra had ever dealt her—if Kyra had ever previously dealt her a smile at all.

"Well done," Kyra declared as Lan and Louise boarded their PEAR.

Kyra and Alicia followed in the next PEAR.

It was a bizarre feeling, arriving to the Lunar Grand. For some reason it felt, to Louise, as if she was simply turning up for another day at work; like she was once more about to be put into service as Costantino Zito's personal guide around a resort she had little real knowledge of herself.

They alighted their respective PEARs and all four of them ventured across the lobby to the lifts.

Louise was certain that she had left her stomach behind in the Basements.

For the first time, she became acquainted with The Full Moon Lounge.

Like Mackenzie's office, the walls were all windows, peering out across the entirety of the Celestial Stays Dome. This time, though, there were none of the individual room dividers. The entire room was open-plan, and, Louise fathomed a guess, designed for events such as this one.

As she took in the seats, their backs to her, and the royal-blue carpet which led up the aisle to the podium, she couldn't help but be brought in mind of some feverish wedding dream she'd had years ago. It had featured her, and some, unknown figure. His face had been steeped in shadow. On waking, she couldn't have said anything about the person in her dream other than the unshakeable, inexplicable knowledge that it *wasn't* Alex Barn.

With Lan now falling behind, into file with Alicia and Kyra; Louise felt her whole body go rigid.

She wondered if she was now feeling more tension racking her muscles than when she'd strived to track down Alex Barn. As she took in the audience, and her eyes settled upon Fiona among the crowd, she sensed Alicia creeping up beside her; her lips brushing her earlobe.

"Barn was sent back down a couple of days ago—*really low key* . . . She wanted to stick around, though; wanted to thank you personally . . . see you get your comeuppance, I expect."

When Louise met Fiona's gaze, Fiona gave her a delicate smile, nothing more than the slightest of expressions. Louise could already see that the bruise which Alex had given her on her cheek had retreated back; that there wouldn't be any lasting mark.

Louise took the final few steps to the podium, fixing her attention on the Supervisors seated up on the raised platform. From the five of them, she picked out Supervisor William Duval, and, of course, Supervisor Mackenzie Angliss.

As she stood up above the assembled group of people—no more than fifty or sixty of them—she couldn't help wondering about the Shuttle Alex Barn had been sent back to Earth on . . . and if it was the same as the one which Njhay had been intending to take back.

With that thought on her mind, she scanned the audience, searching for Njhay's face.

On her initial pass, she couldn't locate it. And she felt as if she might have a migraine coming on.

There was no time for her to reconcile these feelings, though, because her attention was soon being called upon by Mackenzie Angliss.

She wished for Louise to stand beside her at the podium.

Louise had never been anything approaching a confident public speaker—it wrung her stomach to think about *all* those sets of eyes peering up at her. As if reading her mind, Mackenzie leaned into her and said, "Just smile and wave, and say 'thank you'; that's all that's required."

Mackenzie made it sound so easy.

Mackenzie stood up above the room, and addressed the assembled crowd. "Ladies and gentlemen, we are all here today to celebrate a wonderful act of valour from one of our beloved members of staff." She flashed Louise a sidelong glance. A smile flickered across her lips.

It did very little to settle Louise's nerves.

Mackenzie continued, "Called into action—and taking *great* initiative when it was needed most—Louise Williams stood firm, used her ingenuity." She paused, an apparent moment for group reflection. "In short, Louise Williams showed herself to be nothing short of a *hero*."

Louise was fairly certain that her blushes could be seen back on Earth . . .

"And so," Mackenzie went on, "it is with *great* pride that I, on behalf of Celestial Stays—"

The whole room becoming distracted by something happening at the other end, Mackenzie came to a sudden halt in her speech.

Louise followed the group gaze, trying to work out what the fuss was about.

Her heart swelled up to her throat and beat there furiously, because, as she stood up on the platform, observing the commotion at the doors, she noticed Njhay García—*her* Njhay—treading through the gap. Not that it was Njhay who had drawn the interest.

There was someone else.

Louise's eyes flashed over Njhay's for a fraction of a second, but she drew in those gorgeous, bronze-green irises; felt that they blazed their hue upon her imagination.

Whenever she closed her eyes from now on she would see them always.

As Louise stood firm on the platform, feeling as if she was exposed to the elements—to a particularly fierce winter storm back on Earth—she tried to make sense of what she was seeing.

Of the no-nonsense woman, dressed in a smart, royal-blue trouser suit.

Karolin Köhler.

The owner of Celestial Stays.

Just as she appeared in the media, her hair was clippered short to show off only the bristles of her sugar-coloured roots. Her emaciated figure—the speculation of so many gossip rags—seemed even more extreme; even *fiercer* in real life.

Was this real life?

Louise felt a great urge to pinch herself.

To see if she could stop herself dreaming.

Before she really knew what was happening, Karolin Köhler—*Frau Köhler*—locked eyes with her. With a slight smile, she ducked her head and marched toward the platform—*toward Louise*—her high heels clicking smartly as she did so.

As she went along, Louise couldn't help but notice how Frau Köhler's shoes were constantly shimmering, constantly changing colour; like a butterfly's wings. It was a hypnotic effect, similar to the one which Louise witnessed whenever she put on Alicia's dress.

Soon enough, Frau Köhler was standing up on the raised platform, beside Louise, the whole room now steeped in silence. As if there was nobody in the room except for Louise and Frau Köhler herself, Frau Köhler turned into Louise and whispered—in a hoarse, yet intimate voice—with only the hint of a German accent, "Good work."

Frau Köhler then swept into Louise, placing a kiss on either one of her cheeks.

As if nothing at all had transpired, Frau Köhler turned away from Louise. She shifted her attention onto the audience, all of them pinned in their seats. *Stunned.*

In the end, it was Costantino who Louise first saw rise up.

Red-cheeked, beaming from ear to ear.

He started to clap.

Firmly.

Slowly.

As if setting the rhythm for the rest of the room.

Just like the leader of men he was, the audience followed suit, rising out of their seats.

The clapping rose both in volume and rhythm.

Louise felt each one of the slapping pairs of palms sending a tremor down her spine; causing her gut to clench tightly. It was almost as if lightning danced in her veins.

When the applause finally died down, and the audience had

taken their seats, Frau Köhler addressed the room . . . though Louise didn't hear anything of what she said.

Truth be told, she'd become fixated on the fact that Njhay García had managed to sidle up alongside her. He stood so close that she felt his warm breath on the side of her neck.

What she wouldn't give to be away from here . . .

What she wouldn't give to be *away* with Njhay right now . . .

With other thoughts on her mind, Louise nearly missed the moment when Frau Köhler pinned the medal onto her dress. It took Louise another moment still to realise that it was only a virtual representation; and that the fabric would remain unharmed.

Whenever Louise chose to—whenever the situation required it —she could dial up the medals she had earned while in the service of Celestial Stays to be shown on the breast pocket of her overalls.

After another round of applause, Louise felt Njhay's hand clamp about her own. As she tried to recapture her senses, she was aware of Njhay tugging her away—helping her to *escape* . . .

As she passed by the assembled audience, she caught a wink off Costantino Zito; and a hearty pat on the back from Wendy. She wondered whether or not Wendy had been told the truth, about how Louise really wasn't worthy in any way of this honour . . . of having met Frau Köhler.

That she'd had great help from others . . .

But as that thought entered her mind, she couldn't help but wonder about the seating arrangements; about how Wendy was sat beside Costantino—and *were* they holding hands?

Njhay tugged Louise onward before she could see for sure.

When they got free of the Full Moon Lounge, Louise was convinced that she *had* truly escaped, but—as always seemed to be the way—there was still a catch to be had.

This time it was in the form of someone calling her back.

She turned to look.

Saw that it was Mackenzie.

She must've sprinted down the aisle to catch up with them.

Not that she showed any outward signs of being flustered if she had indeed done so.

Mackenzie shifted a quick glance to Njhay, and Louise was surprised to note that it wasn't all fire and brimstone . . . perhaps things between them had thawed at last; although Louise supposed that it would be difficult to stay angry with him when he appeared to be on personal terms with Frau Köhler herself.

"A quick word with Louise?" Mackenzie asked Njhay. "Alone?"

Relenting his hold on her hand, Njhay seemed almost to drift away from Louise. She watched him tread his way down the corridor, only turning his back to her when he needed to go around the corner. Already Louise could feel her mind going wild at the prospect of what was to come; not just *now* but in the future . . . because one thing was beyond doubt; the future *was* theirs . . .

Louise turned back to Mackenzie.

And Mackenzie brought the doors to the Full Moon Lounge shut with a smart *clack*.

She smiled widely. "So," she said, "did you work it all out?"

"Work *what* all out?" Louise replied.

Mackenzie rolled her eyes as if Louise was being a dunce . . . as far as Louise knew, she *was* being a dunce . . .

"This was all a test—don't you see that now?"

Louise furrowed her brow. "You mean you set this all up—all this stuff about *Alex Barn* coming up to the Moon?"

Another eye-roll. "Come on, blue eyes, you know what I'm talking about . . . I don't happen to believe in cosmic coincidence—nothing of the sort—but can't you stretch to thinking that there *just might've* been something working for you . . . something *urging* you to tie off all the knots in your past?"

Louise took a long few seconds to think.

She wasn't sure at all what to say.

Wasn't sure at all what to believe.

"All it took was a shove," Mackenzie continued, "a little *responsibility*, and it seems that fate did all the rest." Now she nodded to the corner behind which Njhay had vanished. "It was up to you how you would deal with it—how you would resolve all of those, uh"—Mackenzie winced—"*hate* the word . . . but it helped you to resolve all those *issues*."

Louise supposed that in a large way, things *had* worked out.

She had tried to run, and been incapable of doing so.

She had been discovered—*found out* . . . but, most important of all, she had faced up to the truth.

And she had embraced her future.

"Go on, then, blue eyes," Mackenzie said, giving Louise a fond pat on the bottom. "I guess Specky'll be waiting for you; though what you see in him *I* can't quite imagine."

Louise took a few steps away from Mackenzie, and then, a thought striking her, she halted.

She turned back around.

Met Mackenzie's fierce, brilliant-green eyes.

"Thanks," she said. "Thanks for everything."

Mackenzie rolled her eyes yet again. "Hurry up, girl, before I have to get Security to escort you from the premises."

With a grin, Louise disappeared around the corner.

They didn't speak until they'd got into the PEAR and were heading away from the Lunar Grand.

Louise was feeling so stirred up by the entire ceremony that she couldn't quite bring herself to look Njhay directly in the eye. When he squeezed her hand, she just about plucked up the courage to slip him a sidelong glance.

"There's something I have to tell you," he said.

"What?" Louise replied, feeling her heart flutter.

"About Frau Köhler—about her coming here."

Louise blinked away her daze, tried to stop the corners of her vision from going all fuzzy.

"You see," Njhay continued, "she didn't make the journey *just* to congratulate you on your heroics." He jerked his head to indicate the Lunar Grand, disappearing quickly over their shoulders. "There *was* the other matter . . . the one concerning Costantino Zito. From what Frau Köhler was telling me on the journey over, she's just had the most hectic week; unable to clear her schedule . . . the best she could manage was to fit in an impromptu meeting on the Shuttle back to Earth." He waggled his head back and forth. "But—to get on the Shuttle back to Earth—she had to *leave* first . . ."

Louise wondered if she should feel somewhat offended at this revelation; but, since she really wouldn't have been able to do it without all the help she'd had, she knew that *being offended* would be ridiculous. She just grinned back at him. "I have to admit I was *more* shocked that you seem to be well acquainted with Frau Köhler—that you seem very much at *ease* in her company."

Njhay blushed a little. He looked away.

Across the lunar plains.

"Well," Njhay continued, "we all have our dirty secrets, huh?"

"I suppose it bodes well for your future relationship with Mackenzie, at least."

Njhay looked back at Louise, shrugged. "Oh, we get along . . . in a *way*."

They flew on in the PEAR for another long few quiet moments.

When it became obvious that Njhay was going to say nothing of what had happened—of the choice he'd made—Louise decided that it all came down to her. "So," she began, "you're really willing to put your work on the line—to put your work *in the back seat*—just because you got all smitten over some watery bag of skin and bones?"

Njhay went pensive for several seconds and Louise regretted her somewhat direct, playful tone.

She knew—for Njhay—his work was a long way from being subject matter for humour.

However, when he turned back into her, she was surprised to see that he was smiling all over.

And that his eyes—beyond the lenses of his glasses—seemed to be twinkling. "I guess you could say that I've spent a long time staring at stuff close up; working out how it all goes together, how things *tick*." He paused, turned his attention back out of the PEAR's visor, to their destination, the Lunar Caverns appearing on the horizon. "Now I'd say it's time to put everything I've learned into practice." He glanced back at Louise. "Time for me to put up, or shut up . . ."

And, as the PEAR descended on the Lunar Caverns landing strip, Louise felt as if she was tingling all over. As if she had finally found what she'd been looking for all this time.

Love?

Of course . . . but that wasn't all . . . that wasn't *enough*.

And what it *exactly* was she'd found, she couldn't quite say.

Not even to herself—not even within her own mind.

But she had found it all the same.

As the PEAR descended the final few metres to the landing strip, she leaned into Njhay, pressed her lips to his. And they kissed; softly, sweetly.

And then with *passion*.

THE END

AUTHOR'S NOTE

Thank you for taking the time to read one of my books. If you would like to hear about my latest releases you can sign up for my newsletter here: www.essiepowers.com

Thanks for reading!

Essie Powers

Lovers' Crescent
The First Lunar Lovescape Novel

www.ingramcontent.com/pod-product-compliance
Lightning Source LLC
Chambersburg PA
CBHW03121226O626
47169CB00007B/2028